"*Red Wolf* depicts an unquestionably shameful part of our history about which today's children should be informed. The novel serves that purpose while reinforcing our feelings of outrage and disgust."

— *Quill & Quire*

"Jennifer Dance has come howling out of the wilderness … and I'm deeply impressed."

— Joseph Boyden, Giller Prize–winning author of *Through Black Spruce*

"Children and young adults alike will want to read Jennifer Dance's novel on the intertwined stories of a wolf and a First Nation boy. It is exactly the sort of story I loved when I was a boy."

— James Bartleman,
Former Lieutenant Governor of Ontario

"Jennifer Dance's *Red Wolf* is a heartrending, relentlessly compelling novel about the impact of the Indian Act of 1876 and the residential schools system upon indigenous cultures."

— *Canadian Materials*

"There are things that non-natives do not understand about our culture. This book will help with the understanding."

— Chief Arnold General, Confederacy Chief from
the Onondaga tribe, Six Nations

Dance's first novel addresses a horrific historical period and details *Red Wolf*'s harsh awakening in painful, hard-hitting scenes ... readers will finish with a strong sense of the abuses suffered by natives at the hands of settlers.

— *Publisher's Weekly*

Poignantly written from the perspective of both boy and wolf, [*Red Wolf*] brilliantly encapsulates the fear, alienation and hopelessness felt by a child who is powerless against a system which seeks to annihilate his heritage, spiritual beliefs and family ties.

— *Stouffville Free Press*

RED WOLF

JENNIFER DANCE

DUNDURN
TORONTO

Editor: Allister Thompson
Project Editor: Laura Harris
Design: Jesse Hooper
Printer: Webcom

Library and Archives Canada Cataloguing in Publication

Dance, Jennifer, author
    Red Wolf / by Jennifer Dance.

Issued in print and electronic formats.
ISBN 978-1-4597-0810-5 (pbk.).--ISBN 978-1-4597-0811-2 (pdf).--ISBN 978-1-4597-0812-9 (epub)

    1. Wolves--Juvenile fiction. 2. Ojibwa Indians--Juvenile fiction. 3. Native peoples--Canada--Residential schools--Juvenile fiction. I. Title.

PS8607.A548R43 2014   jC813'.6   C2013-902962-1
                                             C2013-902963-X

2   3   4   5   18 17 16 15 14

 Conseil des Arts du Canada / Canada Council for the Arts   Canada    ONTARIO ARTS COUNCIL CONSEIL DES ARTS DE L'ONTARIO

We acknowledge the support of the **Canada Council for the Arts** and the **Ontario Arts Council** for our publishing program. We also acknowledge the financial support of the **Government of Canada** through the **Canada Book Fund** and **Livres Canada Books**, and the **Government of Ontario** through the **Ontario Book Publishing Tax Credit** and the **Ontario Media Development Corporation**.

Care has been taken to trace the ownership of copyright material used in this book. The author and the publisher welcome any information enabling them to rectify any references or credits in subsequent editions.

J. Kirk Howard, President

The publisher is not responsible for websites or their content unless they are owned by the publisher.

Printed and bound in Canada.

VISIT US AT
Dundurn.com | *@dundurnpress* | *Facebook.com/dundurnpress* | *Pinterest.com/dundurnpress*

Dundurn	Gazelle Book Services Limited	Dundurn
3 Church Street, Suite 500	White Cross Mills	2250 Military Road
Toronto, Ontario, Canada	High Town, Lancaster, England	Tonawanda, NY
M5E 1M2	L41 4XS	U.S.A. 14150

*May this story open hearts and minds
to the history of Canada
and the long suffering of our First Nations people.
May it be used to restore relationships
and increase peace, understanding, and compassion
among our nation's youth.*

REQUIEM

There was a time long ago,
when wolf and man lived wild and free,
When the white-skins lived far away,
across the Salt Water.
The woods were big then and the forests thick.
Elk and moose were plentiful,
the rivers clear and full of fish.
Counselled by the wisdom of the old ones
and guided by the spirit
We lived in harmony with Mother Earth,
Wolf and man together, yet apart.

There was a time before the loggers cut the great
pines and floated them down the rivers,
Before the traders used our furs and skins to clothe
the white ones across the Big Water,
Before they made us believe that our ways were evil
and our wisdom was foolishness,
Before they controlled us, contained us,
tamed us, restrained us,
Before the diseases, the guns,
the metal traps, the poison bait.
There was a time before we were savages,
Wolf and man together, both.

There was a time long ago …

PROLOGUE

The boy was tied to the courtyard post by his wrists. The rest of the students had to gather around and watch, as if the whipping was a pow-wow at the summer camp of The People. The whip was made of rawhide strips, each with a knot at the end. They ate into the flesh of his back and coiled around his ribcage. It was worse than any pain he had ever felt, but he bit down on his lip until he tasted blood and didn't cry out. The other boys were silent until the very end, and then a strange thing happened: one started to stomp his boot on the ground in a slow, mournful rhythm, like a drumbeat. Another boy picked up the rhythm, and another, and another, until every boy in the school stomped as one, until the ground pulsed, until the master had shouted himself hoarse.

CHAPTER ONE

The Algonquian Wilderness
Ontario, Canada
1885

The men slowly reached for their rifles, eyes searching through the lengthening shadows. They appeared calm, almost serene, but the moment they set eyes on the wolves, fear had tainted their sweat. Tall-Legs had discerned the change. He signalled Tika and the pups to drop to the ground. The Uprights he had encountered in his six years of life were not a threat to him, or he to them. They didn't have the teeth, claws, and speed of his kind, or the formidable antlers and hind legs of the moose or elk. But these Uprights were different. Their pungent odour burned his nostrils. The hackles rose along his spine and his heart beat faster. However, hunger gnawed at his stomach and the meat that lay on the trestle table was tempting. He crouched low, his sensitive nose taking in every detail.

"The big one's mine," the lumberjack drawled, his hand inching toward the rifle that was propped at his side. "Nice and slow. Don't scare 'em off."

Tall-Legs turned to flee.

The bullet caught him in the ribcage, the impact arcing him into the air. He yelped and thudded to the ground, legs twitching. With explosions reverberating around him, one pup whirled and bolted. He had covered a hundred yards before he realized he was alone. He crouched to wait for his family, peering back toward the camp. Everything was still, but his nose and ears told him that something terrible had happened. His paws wanted to flee, but he needed his mother. Taking advantage of the tree cover, he slunk toward her.

Tika lay on her side, her head turned toward him, her yellow eyes demanding that he not approach. He flattened himself on the forest floor, his coat melding with the underbrush, one of his ears pointing skyward in a triangle, the other folded in half. He rested his head on his paws and whimpered softly.

One of the Uprights moved warily toward Tall-Legs and kicked the big wolf in the ribs. The pup cringed, but Tall-Legs made no movement and no sound.

"There's a good pelt on this one. I'll set to skinnin' him after supper."

The smallest pup of the litter lolled with his head resting on his sister's hindquarters. The third pup lay alone. An Upright approached them and kicked each one. The pup with the crooked ear flinched, but his siblings didn't leap up and run away. They remained still and silent.

"The pelts on these young 'uns won't be worth much. They're too small, not worth the effort to skin."

"We still need the tails for the bounty."

"Yeah, just cut the brushes off."

Crooked Ear heard the crunch of blade on bone then his sister's tail flew through the air, landing with barely a thud on the ground by the tents, the smell of her blood mingling with the choking scent of gunfire.

Another Upright warily approached Tika. "This one's still alive!" he shrieked, leaping away like a frightened hare.

Tika was gazing into Crooked Ear's eyes when the final bullet tore through her body, lifting her slightly from the ground. Crooked Ear turned and fled.

"There's another one!"

The lumberjacks unleashed a hail of bullets.

Crooked Ear raced into the darkness of the forest.

All night he ran, instinct leading him to the protected places where the moon barely reached the forest floor. He no longer ran with the playfulness of youth. His puppy days were over. By daybreak

13

his pads were sore and his muscles ached. With heaving flanks, he quenched his thirst at a stream. A tree had blown over, wrenching a large bundle of roots from the earth, leaving a sandy hollow in the ground. He collapsed into it, tucking his nose to his flank and encircling his body with his tail. But even as he slept, his legs still ran, and he whimpered and yelped.

When he awoke, the day was done and darkness was once more settling over the forest. Bounding onto the trunk of the fallen tree, he threw back his head and howled, straining to hear any far-off reply from his pack, but only the hoot of an owl answered his call.

He was alone.

Softly jumping back to the forest floor, he paced in circles, head to the ground, nose urgently snuffling through the dried needles. He scrabbled at a rotting log until it disintegrated and beetles scurried in all directions. He pounced on one, then another, his indecisiveness allowing each to get away. Probing the remainder of the log, he unearthed a nest of plump white larvae. He curled back his lips and daintily picked up a fat grub in his front teeth. Deciding they were edible, he devoured all of them.

The hollow under the fallen tree still retained his odour and warmth, and he stayed there for some time. He heard the squeak of a mouse, but it flew through the sky in the talons of an owl. Settling silently on a pine branch, the bird swivelled its head and peered at the wolf. With a blink of its enormous eyes, it gulped the mouse down. Only the tail remained, dangling from the owl's beak before dancing through the pine fronds to the forest floor. Crooked Ear pounced and swallowed. Then he was running again.

With each rise of the moon his pace slowed. Grubs and small rodents did not stave off his hunger. He inhaled the different scents, separating one from another, identifying them, judging their distance. One made him drool. His paws followed his nostrils until he saw a mallard in the wetland. He crouched in the rushes and advanced on his belly, but when he lunged, the duck rose up on beating wings, its webbed feet treading the air, and Crooked Ear sank into the shallows with nothing more than a mouthful of feathers.

He recognized another delicious smell. The rabbit moved toward him with rocking hops, nibbling the grass. It stopped abruptly. For a fraction of a heartbeat it tried to bolt for cover, but Crooked Ear's jaws closed on its neck. Within a minute nothing remained.

Fate, it seemed, had brought Crooked Ear to the summer territory of The People. He had picked up the scent of Upright miles away, not the frightening odour of lumberjacks and their exploding sticks, but the gentler smell of those who had lived at Clear Lake where he had been born. He howled, but there was no reply.

The People heard his cry, but were too preoccupied to indulge in wolf talk the way they had in the past. They were worried about the pale-faced people moving up from the south, cutting down the great white pines. Travellers told stories that seemed impossible to believe: tales of limbless tree trunks being dragged away by teams of horses and floated down the river to another world; accounts of severed stumps, the girth of ten men; reports of a vast dead land where there was no birdsong, no chittering of squirrels and chipmunks, no deer, no elk, nothing! Nothing except the strangers who wanted to take all the land for themselves and their four-leggeds.

Night after night The People sat around campfires discussing the latest news, trying to reach a decision about what they should do. They sat in big circles and small. They smoked, sang, drummed, and prayed. For generations they had been able to talk and listen until everyone was in agreement, but the more they talked, the more obvious it became that there was little agreement and that nobody knew what to do.

Crooked Ear was afraid to approach the pack of The People uninvited, yet he could not move on.

He paced the periphery of their territory, howling each night and listening for a reply that would invite him to draw near. When his forlorn call was answered, he bolted toward the howl and slithered to a stop in front of a small Upright.

Boy and wolf had not met face-to-face before, but each had a vague sensation that they knew the other. More than two moons had come and gone since they had both lived at Clear Lake, the wolf in the forest on the ridge, the boy in the winter camp on the beach below. It had been a crisp, clear night, right after the spring elk hunt, when wolf and human bellies were fuller than they had been all winter. The moon had risen and the sound of drumming pulsed across the ridge. The wolves had trotted to the outcrop of smooth ancient slabs that tilted toward the crest of the ridge and had listened to the strains of The People. Then, in a tradition as old as the rocks on which they stood, the alpha had thrown back his head and howled. The sound travelled easily through the still night air. The People heard and responded.

Crooked Ear had weaved through the pack that night and trotted to the highest spot on the ridge. Silhouetted against the star-studded sky and clearly distinguished by his ears, one pointing like a triangle to the sky, the other folded in half, the young wolf had thrown back his head and given his first puppy howl. Down on the beach, close to the fire, wrapped in his grandfather's blanket, the boy had cupped his hands around his mouth and howled a reply.

Now, face-to-face with the child, the young wolf bowed down on his front legs, haunches pointed skyward, lowered ears and waving tail gesturing submission and friendship.

HeWhoWhistles blocked his son from running toward the wolf pup. "He is small, but his teeth are sharp."

"Where is his mother?" Red Wolf asked.

"If she was close, she would speak," HeWho-Whistles replied. "I fear she is dead."

Crooked Ear rolled onto his back, exposing his vulnerable soft belly to the new pack. It was a gesture that The People understood. "He says that he will not harm us. He wants to be friends."

HeWhoWhistles approached the young wolf slowly and squatted a few feet away, but when he reached out to stroke the pup's head, Crooked Ear scrambled to his feet and jumped back.

Compassion filled HeWhoWhistles' heart. "He is starving. Look at his ribs!"

Red Wolf tugged at his father's hand. "Can we feed him?"

"Yes, son, the hunting has been good. We have meat. Go get some."

When the child returned with chunks of venison, it didn't take long for the pup to eat from his hand. Then, with his hunger satisfied, he leaned his head into the gentle touch of the small human. For the first time in weeks the pup was content.

The days were warm and long and Crooked Ear's rough, malnourished puppy fur was replaced by the sleek coat of a healthy juvenile. His loneliness vanished along with the hunger in his belly. He was as comfortable with the small Upright as he had been with his brothers and sister, rubbing against him, pushing his head under the soft hairless hands, licking the smooth flat face, and encouraging him to romp like a wolf pup. The boy understood the games but yelped louder than any wolf pup when Crooked Ear nipped or scratched him. The noise startled Crooked Ear so much that he soon learned to play with soft paws and gentle mouth.

Crooked Ear was cautious around the other Uprights. They were unpredictable. They might ignore him, or they might run at him waving their arms and shouting. Sometimes they hurled sticks and stones in his direction. When that happened, he ran into the forest. He caught mice and, if he was lucky, a rabbit or a grouse, but after a while he returned to the human pack, slipping in and out of the shadows and flattening himself into the undergrowth until his senses told him that it was safe to go to the boy.

At nighttime when The People went into their dwellings, He Who Whistles sent Crooked Ear away. "The wolf is a wild creature," he told his son. "He must to learn to take care of himself so he can live wild and free, the way the Great Spirit intended. He has his own path to walk and we must let him find it."

But when all was still, Crooked Ear crept back. He listened for the rhythmic breathing of the family and lay down against the wall of the *wiigwam*, closest to where the boy slept. At dawn, before The People stirred, he stole back into the bush and waited patiently until the boy came looking for him.

Crooked Ear had become accustomed to the smells of The People, but one day his nostrils quivered at an unfamiliar odour. He didn't like it. He whined softly. The People didn't seem alarmed by the smell, and the boy ignored his warning, so Crooked Ear took refuge in the forest.

Red Wolf was the first to see the stranger as he rode into camp. But it was the horse that captured his attention, not the heavyset man or the dog that accompanied them. The child had never seen such a beautiful creature. Its coat gleamed in the sunlight like beech leaves in autumn, and its mane flowed over its neck and shoulder, like a waterfall.

The man heaved himself from the saddle, hitched the horse to a tree and, moving with the discomfort of one who had spent too many hours in the saddle, approached the gathering group of people.

The boy ignored his father's command to sit in the circle. Instead, he stood close to the horse, captivated, as it delicately tugged leaves from the tree and worked to get them past the heavy metal bit. Green slobber frothed from the animal's lips and a sodden mess fell to the ground. Red Wolf laughed.

The stranger was a white-skin, but he spoke in Algonquian, a language that had the same roots as their own *Anishnaabemowin*, and was not hard for The People to understand. He told them he was the government Indian agent, and that loggers would soon be moving into the area. He said they must pack up their *wiigwams* and leave immediately.

"We live on this land," the chief stated. "They cannot cut trees here. We hunt and —"

"The land's been sold," the agent interrupted.

"Sold?" the chief asked, questioning the others as well as the stranger. "Our fathers and our fathers' fathers have lived here for generations."

The Indian agent brandished a paper. "This is the title to the land. It says here that we own the land and you don't."

The People passed the paper from one to the other, confusion on their faces.

The chief tossed the paper to the ground in disdain. "These scratchy lines mean nothing to us."

"This is a deed," the agent said, retrieving the document and dusting it off. "It might mean nothing to you, but it means everything to real people. It's legal. Settlers with lawful title are ready to move onto the land. You get out, or these trees will fall on you."

"This is the land of The People, *Anishnaabe*," the chief announced firmly.

The others agreed, anger simmering in their voices.

The agent held up his hands, revealing the gun holstered on his hip. "Go to the reserve. You will each have your own piece of land. You can build proper homes. You can hunt, farm, do whatever you like. The land will be yours, and nobody will ever be able to move you on again."

"Why should we move to a new place? Our ancestors have lived and died here since time began," one man said.

"Their bones rest in this soil. We cannot leave their spirits here!" added another.

"If we go to this new place, maybe the fishing will not be good."

"Maybe the herds will not pass by."

The Indian agent realized that he was not convincing these people. "The government will give you money to buy food. You won't ever go hungry in the winter." He seemed to have struck a chord with a few of the people.

"There's even going to be a school. Education

is the way to advancement in the modern world. It's the future."

There were a few nods.

The conversation grew louder and more animated, but Red Wolf didn't hear it. He had unhitched the reins and was leading the horse to a patch of grass. Suddenly the air was filled with a strident voice.

"Where's my horse? Who took my horse?"

Frantically looking around, the Indian agent spotted the rump of the chestnut gelding disappearing into the distance, its long golden tail swishing from side to side. A small boy walked alongside the horse. Outraged, the agent broke into a shuffling run, flapping his arms and grunting with the effort. The dog joined the fray, bounding ahead and barking with excitement.

"Stop! Horse thief!" the Indian agent yelled over and over.

Red Wolf stopped, wondering what all the commotion was about. "The horse is hungry," he explained. "I take him where the grass grows best."

"Have your parents not taught you to respect other people's —" the agent searched for the word in Algonquian but there was not one, so he used the English word "— property?"

"What is 'property'?" Red Wolf enquired.

"Owning things! That horse is for me and nobody else, especially not you. You can't just walk off with other people's property."

The boy raised his head and looked squarely into the eyes of the white man. They were unlike any eyes he had seen before, the colour of a pale blue winter sky, fringed with lashes like dried grass.

"Everything is for everyone," Red Wolf said.

"How old are you, Horse Thief?"

The child frowned.

The man rephrased the question in a manner that the boy understood. "How many summers have you seen?"

"Five, I am told. And I am not a horse thief. I was just —"

"Five, eh? You'll be in school soon. Then you'll learn some respect."

Gathering up the reins, the agent pulled himself into the saddle and wheeled the horse around. "I won't forget you, Horse Thief!" he shouted, kicking the gelding forcefully with his heels. The horse flattened its ears and bounded into a canter. "We'll meet again, soon. And then I'll teach you a lesson."

CHAPTER TWO

The People were divided. Some wanted to migrate further north, hoping to find another area that was rich with game and fish, a place where the white man would never come.

"There is no such place," others said.

Voices were strident as everyone tried to make his or her point.

"Many white-skins are coming, more than all of our people."

"They are greedy."

"They want everything for themselves."

"Why do they cut down the trees that hold all of creation together?"

Nobody knew.

A woman whose weathered face bore the signature of a long life of hardship struggled to stand. Gradually the discussion stopped, everyone waiting to hear the old woman's wisdom.

"For the sake of the young ones, go to this place they call 'reserve,' where the children will never be hungry. The Great Spirit teaches us to care for everyone, the old ones who will soon leave our *wiigwams* and go to meet the Ancestors; the young ones who have recently come into our *wiigwams*, filling us again with love and hope; and the generations in between. Today it is hard to know what is best for us all. So I ask you to choose what is best for the children. *They* will carry the life of The People forward. For their sake, I beg you, please do not go where the snows will be deeper and the winters colder, where the game may not come, and the fish may not swim, where your baby's lusty cries will grow weak and fade to silence. Go to a place where you will have shelter, where, at the end of a long winter, you will still have food to fill your children's bellies."

"But what about The Life?" a man asked. "*Anishnaabek Bemazawin*. The Life of hunting, trapping, and fishing, of gathering the bounty of Mother Earth. The Life to roam throughout the land of our grandfathers?"

"What good is The Life," replied the old woman, "if our children have starved to death?"

For a while there was silence. Even those who opposed the old woman's views gave her the respect she deserved.

But the passion to live off the land was powerful, especially in the young men. Later that evening they gathered in smaller groups, eager to voice their opinions. HeWhoWhistles' was one of reason.

"The pale-faced one is asking us to make our mark on his treaty," he said. "He waves his markings at us and tells us what it means, but we cannot interpret the scratchy lines! Some of you have said that the white-skins are not to be trusted. Should we trust their signs?"

There was a movement of heads. "No."

HeWhoWhistles continued. "We have learned to read the signs of the animals, signs that help us and protect us from harm. Now our young ones must learn to read these new signs. Then, in days to come, we will not be deceived."

He sighed heavily. "I do not wish to go to the reserve that they speak of. But I will go. I will go because they will make school for my son."

"We do not need their school. We teach our children everything they must know, just as our fathers taught us."

"We live in different times," HeWhoWhistles replied. "We cannot teach our children the ways of the white-skins. They must go to school and become part of the new world. Our sons and our daughters are the future."

In the end there was no agreement. Some decided to stay and fight the loggers, even though they knew their bows and arrows were poor defense against the exploding sticks of the white-skins. Others decided to leave the area in search of new hunting grounds. But HeWhoWhistles, in the hope of a better future, made his mark on the government paper, and with his wife, his parents, and his son, followed the guide to the reserve.

As the family gathered all its possessions and walked away, Crooked Ear whined softly from his hiding place among the trees. The guide's short fire-stick had not exploded like the long ones in the wolf's memory, but it had that same acrid, burning smell. The intense odour filled his gut with terror and rooted his oversized paws to the spot. He trembled. He wanted to lope after the little Upright, but he couldn't.

As the human procession faded from his eyes, and eventually even from his nose, another type of horror began to gnaw at his stomach: loneliness. With the loneliness came panic. He wanted to run from the invisible enemy, just as he had on that fateful night two moons ago when he had fled from the ground that claimed the blood of his family. Back then weeks of running had left him exhausted, starving, and close to death. Miraculously, he had found the little Upright and had become alive again, but now the little Upright, too, had gone.

His nose searched out the delicate scent of the boy from among the innumerable terrifying smells. When he found what he was hunting for, he snuffled his warm breath into the earth, disturbing the aroma and enriching it. He inhaled deeply. It was comforting. Then, slinking in and out of the shadows, his coat blending perfectly with the undergrowth, he followed the little Upright, who in turn followed the human with the fire-stick. The young wolf had no choice. Neither did the young boy.

After many days, HeWhoWhistles and his family reached a clearing, where *wiigwams* were pitched among log cabins and shacks. At first sight, the area seemed deserted, but soon men and women trickled out of the dwellings and stood watching. There was no joy on their faces, no laughter on their lips. And there were no children. HeWhoWhistles' heart sank.

"Where are the children?" he asked.

"They're at school," the guide replied in Algonquian.

HeWhoWhistles brightened. "Where is school?" he asked, his eyes searching the buildings.

"Over in Bruce County," the man said with a sweeping motion.

"How far?"

"A five-day walk."

"You said it would be *here*! On *this* land. *Our* land."

"You got it wrong! Why would the government build a school here for just a few Indians, and another one somewhere else for a few more? Makes no sense, does it?" The guide didn't wait for an answer. "There's one large school in Bruce County. It's a boarding school. Your boy will live there."

HeWhoWhistles screamed with rage. It was a sound he had never made before.

"Calm down, Indian," the man ordered, drawing his gun. "Step back. Let's talk about this, real calm."

HeWhoWhistles knew the power of the white man's fire-stick. If angered, it would explode and take his life. How would he be able to protect his family then? He did what he thought was best; he backed up and hid his emotion in a stony face.

"He is my son," he stated, his voice flat and controlled.

"You're wrong! The boy's a ward of the government now. He goes to school. That's the law." Algonquian words did not exist for some of the things the man wanted to say, so he interjected English words. "Break the law and we'll lock you up and throw away the key. Understand?"

HeWhoWhistles did not understand. "I put my mark on your paper because you say there would be school *here*. No school, then we leave this place. We go home."

"Too late now," the man said. "You signed! That makes you part of the Indian Act. This is your home now. As for your son, he belongs to the government!"

"No! He will stay with his mother and me. We will teach him the *Anishnaabe* way."

"Don't you understand? You have no parental rights! The Indian Act, sections 113 to 122, took your rights away. The boy goes to school. You should have read what you were signing!"

HeWhoWhistles' rage was barely concealed. He had been deceived. He had made his mark on the white-skins' paper, trusting their spoken words, even though he had been warned that the pale-faced ones were not to be trusted. He had been a fool! And now he was losing his son. He wanted to push his blade deep into the man's gut and twist it upwards, but confronted with the revolver aimed at his chest, he struggled to hold his violent emotion in a motionless body.

StarWoman's eyes were filled with tears, and her voice quivered. "Don't take him from us … please."

The man's heart softened. Thinking the crisis was over, he holstered his gun. "The government intends to educate these children and make them Christians. It will be easier for everyone if you co-operate."

"Who will look after him?" StarWoman asked, panic rising in her throat. "He needs me. He has seen only five summers."

"He'll be treated well. The house-mother at the school cares for the little Indians like they were her own."

"But he is *my* son!" StarWoman protested.

The man's patience was wearing thin. "As I told you before," he said sharply, "you have no choice. The Indian Act says the boy has to go to school. Anyway, it's not forever. You can fetch him home for two months every summer. Apart from that he's the government's responsibility until he's fifteen."

StarWoman lunged at the man, howling like a crazed animal, beating her fists against his chest and clawing at his face. "I will not let you take him, I will not, I will not."

With a firm shove, the man pushed StarWoman away. She stumbled back and fell to the ground in convulsive sobs. He reached for his gun and aimed.

HeWhoWhistles acted without thinking, throwing himself on his wife, covering her and protecting her from the fire-stick that would surely kill her.

The white man's finger trembled on the trigger. He had shot Indians before and hadn't lost sleep over it, but not like this. Not in the back, not when they were already down. Indians were no better than dogs, but he wouldn't even shoot a dog like this.

HeWhoWhistles held his breath, expecting to hear the explosion of the fire-stick and feel the burning stone rip through his back. Seconds passed. Apart from StarWoman's stifled sobs there was silence.

A paper fluttered to the ground and landed by his head. "Here's your pass. You and the boy can leave in the morning. The school term's already started, so don't dawdle. Anyway, you only have ten days; five there, five back. There's a date on the pass. If you're not back by that date, we'll throw you in jail when we catch you. Understand?"

HeWhoWhistles had protected his woman from the fire-stick, but he couldn't protect his son from the government.

CHAPTER THREE

Crooked Ear followed the child and his father for five days, his pads falling softly on the narrow trail, but when the forest ended and the track headed diagonally across a meadow, he would go no further. He needed to feel the protection of the trees. Open spaces made him anxious. So he sat on his haunches just within the tree line, one ear pricked to the sky, the other folded in half, his amber eyes following the two Uprights. The little one ran back to him and buried a wet face into his ruff, but the soothing feeling was not there.

The tall Upright took the little one by the hand and led him into the gentle waves of sun-bleached grass. Crooked Ear trembled and whined, wanting to follow, but the feral part of his nature kept him rooted. The little Upright vanished first, then the tall one disappeared. Their scent hung on the air, and Crooked Ear raised his nostrils to the breeze and inhaled. Then he sat on his haunches and waited.

Red Wolf reached out and clutched his father's hand. In silence they walked the last few miles, their pace slowing until, some ten feet from the gate, they stopped.

"I am frightened," Red Wolf whispered.

Man and boy stared through the iron bars of the gate to the large building that stood in a grassy clearing. It was like nothing they had ever seen; big, solid and symmetrical, with three rows of small barred windows neatly stacked, one on top of the other.

"I don't want to go to school," Red Wolf said, gazing without comprehension at the mandate etched over the main doorway: TO RESCUE THE HEATHENS FROM THEIR EVIL WAYS AND INTEGRATE THEM INTO CHRISTIAN SOCIETY.

"We have no choice," his father replied. "It is the white man's law. You must learn their ways. It is the only hope for The People."

The boy's chin quivered. "I want to go home," he said, the back of his hand quickly wiping a tear from his cheek.

Tears stung HeWhoWhistles' eyes, but he would not allow them to fall.

"It will be exciting for you," he said, forcing a smile, "like going to summer camp! You will have new friends to play with."

Red Wolf remembered how he had felt each spring when his family left their small camp on the beach at Clear Lake and made the annual migration to the larger summer camp in the northern forest. It was exciting to pack the entire contents of their home into canoes and paddle for days across lakes and up rivers, sleeping under the stars, and waking to the calls of loons. He wished he were back in the canoe now, trailing a hand in the clear water, watching his father's muscular shoulders, listening to the quiet dip of the paddle, the slap of a hand on a mosquito, or the rasp of fingernails on bitten flesh. He remembered how eager he had been to sleep in the new summer *wiigwam*, even though it was identical to the winter one, right down to the mats, the furs, and the birch-bark containers that they brought along. But he didn't feel any excitement now, only apprehension and gut-wrenching sadness.

"Soon you will understand the white man's signs just as you understand the signs of the animals," HeWhoWhistles said, "then you will make marks and send them to me."

The child lowered his head and stared at his feet, working the toe of his elk-hide moccasin into the dusty surface of the laneway. "But how will you understand the marks, Father?"

HeWhoWhistles sighed. "I will visit soon … as soon as they let me leave the reserve. Time will pass quickly. Winter will come. And go. And then you will return to us."

The sound of a key turning in a lock brought father and son back to the world around them. They looked through the iron bars of the gate directly into the round face of a man who had not one hair on his head.

"You're late. Very late! Days late!" the man said in stilted Algonquian. "Come. *Biindigek*. Hurry."

He opened the gate and yanked the child through, slamming the bars in the face of HeWhoWhistles and turning the key with a loud clunk.

"I must see where he will be," HeWhoWhistles demanded. "His mother, she must know."

"Come back at the end of June," the man shouted, dragging the child toward the building.

"June?" HeWhoWhistles said.

"When the sun is high in the sky," the man explained. "When the days are long."

"He needs this," HeWhoWhistles protested, offering up an elk-skin pouch.

"Take it home!" the bald man yelled. "And get out of here right now or I'll set the dog on you."

Red Wolf dug in his heels and used all of his strength to resist the force of the big man who was taking him from his father. Impatient with the slow progress, the man gripped the boy's ear and lifted him to his toes. Red Wolf squealed and lashed out blindly with his fists. The man let him go and doubled over, hands between legs, blotches of scarlet spreading up his neck and over his head. Red Wolf dashed toward his father, throwing himself against the locked gate, scrambling to get a foothold, trying to climb up and over.

HeWhoWhistles pointed to the top of the tall gate, where barbed wire lay coiled like a sleeping snake. "The wire has teeth! It will eat your flesh! "

Red Wolf continued scrambling upward. He was inches from the top when the man's powerful arms grabbed him, jerked him away from the gate, and carried him through the school door. He fought to look back at his father. HeWhoWhistles had sunk to his knees and was wailing.

The school door slammed shut. "Listen well," the man growled, tossing Red Wolf against the wall as though he had no more weight than a leaf. "I will talk in your tongue so you will understand. I am Mister Hall. I run things here."

He lowered his voice to a whisper and hissed through crooked yellow teeth. "I can make your life very uncomfortable, or we can be friends. You get to choose. See, it all depends on how you behave. Understand?"

Before he could respond, Red Wolf was shoved into the wall a second time. He gasped, struggling to breathe.

"As far as I'm concerned, you're a worthless Indian," the man said, spittle flying from his mouth along with the mixture of Algonquian and English words. "And it's a waste of everybody's time trying to educate you, civilize you, and integrate you. You'll never be anything but a filthy savage!"

A glob of saliva fell on Red Wolf's shin. It crept along the slope of his foot toward the porcupine quills that his mother had sewn on his moccasin. He watched as though all of this was happening to a different child, a different foot, a different moccasin.

The man released his grip and stepped back a pace, wagging a finger vigorously in the air and barking strange words. "I don't enjoy this job, but it's a good income for me and the wife. So what I'm saying is this —"

Red Wolf struggled to focus on the tip of the finger that was moving closer and closer to his face. And then it happened — he felt himself stretching upward, growing taller and thinner until he was looking down on the man's bald head. He saw sweat gleaming there.

"— don't make my job more difficult, or you'll be sorry."

Red Wolf floated peacefully. Beneath him, the man's meaty fist engulfed the fragile hand of a small boy, a boy whose eyes were wide with fear. Red Wolf noticed the whiskers that sprouted from the man's ears. They were the colour of autumn leaves and he thought it strange that Mister Hall had orange hair on his ears, but none on his head. He wondered if the hair of white-skins changed colour in the autumn and fell from their heads like the leaves fall from the trees.

The man's demeanour softened, his mouth stretching into a grin. "But if you behave yourself, you'll be just fine."

Red Wolf slid back into his own moccasins, but he felt no reassurance from the man's words, and no comfort from the man's smile. The grey-blue eyes did not twinkle with warmth and kindness like those of The People. And, as Mister Hall led him along the corridor, he felt something he had never felt before: dread.

"This is your house-mother, your *wiigwam* mother," Mister Hall said, speaking loudly in stilted Algonquian. "She's my wife, my woman. But you call her Mother Hall. Understand?"

The woman's voice was shrill and she spoke words that had no meaning. "Take off your clothes so I can disinfect you. We don't want your lice and fleas in the building."

Red Wolf stared blankly at her.

"Quickly!"

Her mouth continued to move as she spat sounds into the air. Red Wolf watched, but he didn't understand the words. He noticed the thin, colourless hair that was pulled tightly from her face, creating the illusion that she had no hair at all. He noticed that her long grey skirt was fastened at the waist with a leather belt and that rawhide strips hung from the belt, dangling almost to the ground. The woman fingered them as she spoke. Suddenly, with a flick of the wrist, she sent the strips flying through the air. They snaked around Red Wolf's bare calves with a stinging slap. He jumped away, yelping at the unexpected pain. He bit his bottom lip and wiped away the tears with the back of his hands.

The woman continued to make the strange sounds, her whole face involved in her speech, but Red Wolf kept his eyes focused on her hands, especially the right hand. When it brushed against the rawhide strips, he braced for more stinging pain, but it didn't come. Instead the woman thrust both her hands skyward and looked up. Red Wolf looked up too.

"Good grief!" she exclaimed. "Here's another one that don't speak English, not a single word!"

Slower and louder still, she tried again. "Take ... off ... your ... clothes."

She pulled the soft hide shirt over his head and tossed it into the open lid of the potbellied stove. The fire belched smoke. The child was distraught. He had failed to protect his mother's handiwork and her disappointment weighed on him. He told the

41

woman how hard his mother had worked making the shirt, and how she had made the fringe extra long because he had wanted it that way.

The rawhide strips coiled around his legs and ankles.

"Don't speak that savage language!"

It was fear, not comprehension that made him obey.

Why did Father leave me here? Why doesn't he come and take me home?

The silence was soon shattered by another shrill outburst from the woman. Red Wolf stood immobile and mute. Mother Hall reached out to remove his breechcloth. Red Wolf held on fast, but after a brief struggle the woman won and, except for the wolf's head pendant that hung around his neck on a strip of leather, he was naked.

"Superstitious witchcraft!" she shrieked, snatching the pendant with a force that broke the leather and bruised his neck. She turned to poke at the fire, not noticing that the pendant had slipped from the leather to the floor.

Red Wolf's foot reacted instantly, pushing the pendant under the desk, where it was out of sight. As his bare toes made contact with the carved bone, he remembered when his father had made it. It had been in the days following the summer hunt when the weary hunters had rested and when the women had worked at preparing the meat.

HeWhoWhistles was sitting at the edge of the lake, holding a piece of bone in his palm and running his fingers over it, listening to it, he had said, so he could free the spirit within. But then Grandmother had spoiled everything! Usually Red Wolf enjoyed spending time with the old woman; she told him the names of the plants, the ailments they cured, the colour dye they gave, what was good for brewing tea or flavouring stew. But on this day he had just wanted to sit with his father and watch the magical transformation that was about to happen.

Later, when he returned to his father's side, the pelvic bone of the deer had become the head of a wolf. Red Wolf was thrilled when his father tied it around his neck on a rawhide strip.

Now, naked in front of this stranger, with his hands clasped over his groin, a tear slipped onto his cheek. He didn't notice Mother Hall pick up the shears. Before he had the chance to realize what was happening, both of his braids had been chopped off and tossed into the potbellied stove. The boy was aghast. His hands left his private parts and flew to his head, reaching for the remaining hair that bounced around his ears. He knew hair was sacred! It should be cut only when someone died.

Has Mother died? Is that why Father brought me here? The odour of burning hair filled his lungs and he could no longer hold back the torrent of tears.

"Only babies cry," Mother Hall said, flicking the whip again, but Red Wolf jumped away in time.

She shook the whip toward him, steering him backward to the far side of the room, all the while speaking the language that he couldn't understand. "Stay away from the stove! I've got to wash your hair in kerosene to kill the lice. We don't want you going up in flames and setting fire to the whole building."

He understood the sternness in her voice.

"Shut your eyes," she ordered, closing her own eyes to demonstrate. When the boy obliged, she forced his head over a chipped enamel bowl and poured a strong-smelling liquid over his scalp.

"Keep 'em shut."

His head started to sting. He squeezed his eyes even tighter and tried not to breathe, but tears were choking him and some of the liquid ran into his mouth. It burned. He spat and spat again. When he thought he could stand it no longer he was lifted into a metal tub and warm water was poured over his head. Ignoring his coughing and spluttering, the house-mother lathered his head with soap. Finally, she pulled him out, wrapped him in a towel, and prodded him back toward the stove. For a horrifying second Red Wolf thought that she was going to toss him into the flames. He almost collapsed with relief when he realized that he was just supposed to stand close to the stove to dry.

The woman handed him clean clothes and mimed putting them on. The thick underpants and trousers felt rough and scratchy on his skin, unlike the soft deerskin breechcloth and leggings he had grown up in. He stared blankly at the unfamiliar fasteners on the white cotton shirt.

"It goes like this," Mother Hall said, slipping the tiny button through the equally tiny hole. He clumsily tried to fasten one. "You'll soon be able to do it. Here, put these on your feet."

She helped him lace and tie the brown leather boots. They felt uncomfortable. The rough leather chafed his bare skin. He was unable to stretch and wiggle his toes as he had always done in his moccasins. But worst of all, he could not feel the earth beneath his feet.

"You'll get wool socks when the weather gets cold, and a jacket and cap, too," she said, wrapping a stiff collar tightly around his neck and attaching it with a stud. It was so tight he could barely breathe.

"Now pull the suspenders up over your shoulders, like this. And put your arms into this waistcoat."

Standing back to admire the transformation, the woman smiled. "Good," she said. "You look almost civilized." Without understanding any of the words, Red Wolf knew she was happier now. Her tone was lighter and he felt less threatened. "Now let me straighten things up here and I'll take you to the office."

Red Wolf ran his hands down his new clothes, discovering two deep pockets in his trousers. As soon as the woman turned her back, he snatched up the wolf pendant from under the desk and plunged it into the right pocket. He fingered the smooth bone and traced its outline, seeing the face of the wolf in his mind. The bone became warm to his touch and comforted him. He had this one thing, this one memory of home, and he was determined to keep it at all cost.

Mother Hall finished her chores and turned her attention back to the boy. "Take your hands out of your pocket, boy," she ordered.

He remained still and silent, not risking another slap by confessing that he did not understand.

"Hand," she said, lifting his left hand from his pocket.

The child's heart raced. *Don't let her find my pendant.* Holding out her own large hands, she repeated the word, "Hand."

Red Wolf realized that she wanted him to make the same sound. Tentatively at first, expecting the rawhide strips to wrap around his legs, he said the word.

The woman smiled. "Good," she exclaimed, tousling his new short hair, "that's a start. You'll be talking English in no time. Come on. I'll take you to meet Father Thomas."

CHAPTER FOUR

Father Thomas was sitting at a large oak desk, writing in a ledger with a quill that he dipped into a pot of dark ink. Red Wolf, who was barely taller than the desk, stood on tiptoes to see better.

Blotting his work, the priest stood and peered at the new boy. The boy peered back, fascinated by the two circles of glass balanced in front of the priest's bulging eyes.

"Better late than never," he said, unhooking the wire frame from around his ears and placing the reading glasses on the desk. "George! That's your new name. G-E-O-R-G-E, George."

Red Wolf stared blankly at the strangely dressed man.

The priest spoke louder and touched Red Wolf's chest lightly with his index finger. "George! Understand? You say it ... George."

Red Wolf, relieved to see that the man didn't wear the rawhide strips around his waist, said nothing.

The priest sighed. "We can't keep track of your heathen names, and anyway they're too difficult to pronounce, so from now on your name will be George Grant."

Red Wolf spoke in the language of The People, proudly telling the man in the black robe that his name was *Mishqua Ma'een'gun.* "I am named *Mishqua* for the red of the firelight that shone on my face when I was born. And I am named *Ma'een'gun* for the wolves who announced my birth with their howls. The wolves did not howl to claim territory, or announce a herd was nearby. They did not talk of loneliness, or hunger. They sang a joyful song to celebrate my birth. They said I am their brother and that my name is *Ma'een'gun*: Wolf. *Mishqua Ma'een'gun*: Red Wolf."

He smiled, pleased with himself for telling the story so well.

The priest reached for Red Wolf's hand and turned the palm upward. "This hurts me as much as it hurts you," he said, smacking the ruler down across the unsuspecting child's palm, "but it's for your own good. You have to learn."

Red Wolf snatched his stinging hand away and hid it behind his back. His bottom lip quivered and he wanted to cry, but he suspected that tears would bring more punishment.

The priest placed the ruler back on the desk, rested both hands on Red Wolf's cringing shoulders, and lowered his face to the same level as the child's. "Say George."

The boy copied the sound hesitantly. "Saygeorge."

The priest exhaled. "You'll soon understand. Anyway, your name doesn't really matter. In the school you'll be known by a number. Your number is 366. Understand? I'll write it on your hand so you remember." The child struggled to free his hand from Father Thomas's grasp.

"Don't worry! This won't hurt."

The boy couldn't understand the assurance, so he continued struggling, but this time there was no pain as the man inked numbers onto his flesh.

"You will find things different here," the priest continued. "You will have lessons in the morning and farm work in the afternoon." He looked at the long-case clock that stood in the corner of the room. "Oh, my, it's nearly bedtime. You got here far too late!" He popped his head out of the door and shouted down the corridor, "Mrs. Hall!"

The house-mother promptly appeared with a pile of bedding. Before she shepherded the child from the office, Father Thomas knelt to look Red Wolf in the eye. He reached out as if to take hold of the boy's hands, but Red Wolf was too quick for him and hid them behind his back. The man rested his soft white hands on the boy's shoulders instead and spoke gently. "We are strict, not because we are mean, and not because we want to hurt you, but because you need to learn our language, our civilized ways, our Christian religion. Believe me, it's for your own good. You'll thank me one day. You see, you'll never get to Heaven unless I save your heathen soul."

Red Wolf had absolutely no idea what the priest said.

Red Wolf followed Mother Hall along the corridor, up two flights of wood stairs, along another corridor, and into a long room filled with two rows of rectangular boxes. There was a flurry of activity as boys scampered to them, jumped on top, and pulled grey blankets to their chins. They lay still and silent, their dark eyes staring at Red Wolf as he walked toward the vacant bed.

Mother Hall twisted Red Wolf's arm so that the inked numbers on his hand were the same way up as the painted sign on the wall above the bed.

"Three-six-six," she said. "That's you!"

She quickly unfolded a clean bed sheet and sent it billowing into the air, allowing it to float down onto the horse-hair mattress.

"Watch how I'm doing this," she said. "Next time, you'll do it yourself. I'm not playing house-maid to you." She tucked the corners and sides and smoothed it down, following it with a grey blanket.

She slid the stained pillow into a clean pillowcase and then gave him a nightgown. "Here, take off your clothes and put this on."

Red Wolf still had no comprehension of the words, but he understood what was expected of him. Mother Hall helped him with the shirt buttons and showed him how the day clothes were to be folded. She held the trousers upside down, making them crease down the front. Red Wolf's heart leapt. *The pendant will fall out. She'll see it. She'll hit me. She'll burn it.* But miraculously the pendant defied gravity. Relief washed over him. The trousers were folded and along with his other clothes were stashed in the box under the bed.

"Prayers, boys," Mother Hall ordered.

The boys jumped from their beds and knelt. In unison they slowly recited: "Now I lay me down to sleep, I pray the Lord my soul to keep. If I should die before I wake, I pray the Lord my soul to take. Amen."

"Bed!" Mother Hall ordered.

Red Wolf, who was accustomed to sleeping on a mat or fur laid on the earth, found it strange that he was expected to sleep on this platform in the air, but during the last few hours he had learned not to question things and to move fast when instructed to do something, so taking his lead from the other boys, he quickly climbed onto the bed and pulled the blanket up to his chin.

Mother Hall turned down the wicks of the oil lamps, plunging the room into darkness.

Red Wolf was exhausted and longed to close his eyes and sleep forever. But his mind wouldn't let him go to that place of hiding. Around him boys tossed and turned, molding their bodies into the lumpy mattresses. They snuffled and whimpered and snored, but Red Wolf stared through the vertical bars of the window to the black sky. Before long a half moon rose and in his mind's eye he saw his father. It had been the last night of their trek to the school. *Just the previous night!* It seemed so very long ago. "When you look up and see the moon and the stars, know that we are looking at the same moon and the same stars … and we are loving you."

Tears pricked the corners of his eyes and he yearned with an intensity he had never felt to be back with his father and mother, snuggled under their shared blanket close to the fire. He fought to be the brave boy he knew his father wanted him to be.

HeWhoWhistles' voice spoke again. "Every night before we go to sleep, we will ask Creator to watch over you. Never forget, my son, that *Ma'een'gun* is your brother and your guide. He will help you. And remember the story of your birth."

In this unfamiliar sleeping place, raised above the floor, and without furs or family to keep him warm, Red Wolf tried to hear HeWhoWhistles tell the story of his birth. It was a story that had been told and retold on winter nights when the wind had whistled around the *wiigwam* and snow had blown down the chimney and sizzled in the fire; nights when The People had snuggled under bear skins, singing songs and telling the history of their tribe, going back to the very beginning. But he couldn't concentrate on his father's voice.

A horrifying thought struck him. Had his mother sent him away because he ate too much food? He was always asking for more. He saw StarWoman in his mind's eye, smoothing the long strands of black hair that had fallen loosely around her face, gathering them at the nape and fastening them with sinew so they flowed down her back like a horse's tail. He remembered the worried look on her face when the baskets of rice and smoked meat were empty, when his belly ached and he whined for food. He heard the shortness of her reply, "No," then the softer reassurance that tomorrow HeWhoWhistles would check the traps again and would bring home a rabbit. But tomorrow would come and often there would be no rabbit, and he would complain again. Was that the reason she didn't want him anymore?

He slipped out of bed and in the darkness felt through his clothes until he found the wolf pendant. Cupping it in his hand, he climbed back into bed and drew his knees to his chest, wrapping his whole body around his only possession. "Brother Wolf," he murmured, "help me find my way home."

Finally he slept and dreamed.

"Tell me a story, Mishomis," he asked, nuzzling his face into Grandfather's chest. "The one about Nanabozho … in the beginning …"

"In the beginning," Grandfather started, "Creator made a world of —"

Red Wolf joined in, "Water… wind … Rock … and fire."

"That's right! And to the sun he gave the power to heat and light the earth.

To the earth he gave the power of growth and healing.

To the water he gave purity and renewal.

To the wind he gave music, and the breath of life itself.

After these things, Creator made animals and us, The People, Anishnaabek.

But The People had much to learn about how to live on this earth, about how to —"

"Hunt," Red Wolf chimed in loudly.

"And how to —" Grandfather looked expectantly at the boy.

"Heal?" the child said hesitantly.

"Yes! The Great Spirit needed to teach us about kindness, honesty, and generosity. So He sent a teacher whose name was —"

"Nanabozho!"

"Looking at Nanabozho, you wouldn't know that he was any different from you," the old man continued, "but he was. He was half spirit and half human. His mother was Woman, and his father was the West Wind! And what could Nanabozho do?"

"He could do wondrous things," Red Wolf answered proudly.

The weathered creases on the old man's face deepened and a toothless smile stretched across his open lips. "When Nanabozho walked the earth, Creator sent Ma'een'gun, the wolf, to walk with him, to talk with him and hunt with him."

"They were friends?" Red Wolf suggested.

"Yes, but they were more than friends. Nanabozho and Ma'een'gun became like brothers. But one day when they were hunting together they got so excited that they disobeyed the instructions and they killed more than they needed. They killed just for the fun of it."

"That was bad, wasn't it, Grandfather?"

"Yes, it was," the old man affirmed, the strong, deep tone of his voice disguising the frailty of aging flesh and bones.

"And from that day forward, Creator made Nanabozho and Ma'een'gun, and all their descendants, both wolf and man, walk on separate paths."

"They were not allowed to be friends anymore?"

The old man paused, working his tongue around his few remaining teeth while thinking of a way to answer the child. "It became a different friendship," he finally said. "Ma'een'gun is still our brother. More than that — Ma'een'gun is our spirit guide. But wolves walk one path and we walk another. Sometimes the paths are close together. Sometimes not. Sometimes they go in the same direction. Sometimes not."

The old man lovingly touched his grandson's head, his aged eyes bright with love. "But when we need guidance the spirit wolves are always close by.

"Always."

CHAPTER FIVE

Red Wolf was jolted into consciousness by a loud clanging. With a thumping heart, he clapped his hands over his ears and ran for his mother. He fell from the bed and landed flat on his face on the wooden floorboards, the wolf head pendant falling from his hand and skittering along the floor, disappearing under the next bed. Everyone was looking at him and laughing at him. He knew this even though he lay face down on the floor, but all he was worried about was if anyone had seen the wolf head. He pleaded with it to remain hidden until he could safely retrieve it.

"Silence!" Father Thomas ordered.

The laughter stopped.

Red Wolf scrambled to his feet, the foreign surroundings crashing into him like a charging bull moose. Instantly he was wide awake and terrified. Outside the barred window it was still dark, but in the yellow lamplight he could see the other boys in their nightshirts, kneeling beside their beds, pressing their palms and fingers together.

Red Wolf knelt beside his bed and copied them, but he peeked through narrowed eyes, not wanting to miss any command that might earn him punishment.

Father Thomas, wearing a white nightrobe, was talking in the language that made no sense. He rocked back and forth on his slippered heels, exposing glimpses of blue-grey ankles. He didn't have his ruler with him. Red Wolf followed the priest's upward gaze, wondering who he was talking to up there, but he could see no one. The wooden beams and rafters were more substantial than the slim poles of his birch-bark *wiigwam*, but there was no opening for the smoke from the fire. In fact, there was no fire! Red Wolf had never lived without fire, and the damp cold of the dormitory soon caused him to shiver.

"Aaah-men," the boys said.

Mister Hall, his bald head shining in the lamp-light, entered the dormitory making a drumming rhythm by smacking his walking cane into the palm of his hand. Red Wolf thought that soon there would be singing or dancing. He was shocked when the boys who had wet beds leaned over to touch their toes, upending their bare bottoms. Mother Hall used words to admonish each child, then Mister Hall used his cane, and finally Father Thomas added a blessing. It went like this:

"You filthy boy!" Thwack. "God save your

heathen soul. Amen."

"You disgusting bed-wetter!" Thwack. "God save you from your pagan ways. Amen."

"You good-for-nothing Indian!" Thwack. "God bless you, even though you're an Indian."

In this manner Red Wolf began to understand the English language.

Still in their nightshirts, the boys put on their school boots. Red Wolf fumbled at the trailing laces then hid them down inside the boots against his bare ankles.

"Ablutions!" Mother Hall shouted, choosing a boy to carry the communal night-soil bucket.

Immediately, the children fell into line behind the boy with the pail. Red Wolf brought up the rear, where he imitated the rhythm of their swinging arms and marching feet. The line proceeded out the dormitory, along the corridor, down two flights of stairs, and along a passageway to the side of the building. As soon as the first boy in line pushed open the door, Red Wolf wriggled his nose at the stench then stood aghast at the sight that met his eyes; some twenty boys sat on a long bench that straddled a deep, smelly trench. Their nightshirts were hiked around their waists, and ankle boots, on the ends of bare legs, waved in the air. A boy jumped off the bench and the next in line took his place, then another and another. When it was Red Wolf's turn he didn't move fast enough.

"Hurry up. Get on the throne," the latrine orderly said. "You have two minutes. After that you have to wait until tomorrow." Red Wolf didn't understand the words, though he knew what he was supposed to do. But since the orderly's demeanour was not threatening, since his skin was brown not white, since he held no ruler or leather strips, Red Wolf didn't rush.

"You lost ten seconds already," the youth said, stretching his hand toward Red Wolf and showing him the pocket watch in his palm.

Had Red Wolf's senses not already been in overload, the moving hands of the timepiece would have fascinated him. Instead, he approached the vacant space on the bench and holding his breath peered through the round hole in the wood. It looked very big, and he wondered if he could balance on it without falling through, but the orderly was getting increasingly impatient, so he climbed up, trying not to sit on his nightshirt, and settled his skinny buttocks over the hole.

For the next part of the ablutions routine Red Wolf went to the adjacent washhouse and waited in line again. When it was his turn he hung a bucket over the spigot, then leaned his body weight over the long handle. He was impressed when icy water instantly spewed into the pail, without any sign of a lake or river. He carried the half-filled bucket to where other boys were stripping off their nightshirts and washing their bodies, under the vigilant eyes of Mother Hall. Once again, he watched carefully and copied the others, first picking up a cake of lye soap and a rag, then washing himself in the following order; hands, face, armpits, backside, and feet. Finally a larger rag was used to rub dry.

Throughout this part of the daily routine, Mother Hall repeated a mantra that Red Wolf would later come to understand. "Cleanliness is next to godliness."

After pouring the dirty water down a drain and hanging the rags to dry, the children donned their nightshirts and boots again and marched back to the dormitory to make their beds and put on their school uniforms. While everyone was distracted, Red Wolf scrambled under the bed as though his life depended on it, retrieved the wolf head, and plunged it safely in his pocket. For a few moments he felt much better, but as soon as Mother Hall noticed his untied laces, his stomach tensed again.

"You've got to learn this quickly," she said, bending over and tying a bow. "I can't be leaning over all the time, not with this bad back of mine." Red Wolf strained to see how the woman manipulated the laces, but Mother Hall's spindly fingers moved too fast. Then it was breakfast.

Never had Red Wolf seen a room as large as the refectory, and never had he seen so many boys. They were all wearing the same clothes and the same vacant expression. And they were all silent. A plump woman at the counter ladled food into his upheld bowl. He stared at the thick, lumpy goop, but was soon pushed along by impatient boys and steered toward one of many plank tables.

A booming voice broke the silence. "Let us pray."

Red Wolf copied the other children as they bowed their heads, closed their eyes, and held their hands in the position he had learned that morning.

"Thank you, Lord, for the bounty that you have provided today, for the food which we will now enjoy —"

Red Wolf peeked at Father Thomas. The priest had changed out of his nightclothes and was once again wearing the black robe from the previous day. The boy thought it strange that the robe had no openings at the front. The robes of The People opened down the front. Mister Hall's shirt opened down the front. So did Red Wolf's new school shirt and the shirts of all the other boys. But Father Thomas's robe didn't seem to have any openings, and the stiff white collar that throttled his neck appeared to be the wrong way round, too. Red Wolf wondered if the priest had forgotten the right way to dress himself.

The boy looked at the crossed sticks that hung from the Father's neck. Red Wolf furtively slipped his hand into his trouser pocket and caressed the piece of carved bone, seeing the image of the wolf head through his fingertips. The warmth that came to his fingers as he rubbed them over the bone made him feel warm all over. *My wolf is much nicer than his sticks. Is that why they tried to take it away from me? Do they want it for themselves?*

Finally the boy deduced, correctly, that since the priest was the only one wearing women's skirts, the only one wearing his clothing backwards, and the only one wearing the crossed sticks, Father Thomas must be chief.

Red Wolf's stomach growled. He had not eaten since the previous morning, and he was hungry. Food was in front of everyone, but nobody was eating! They were poised over their bowls, immobile as rock carvings, heads lowered, eyes closed, palms together. Red Wolf ascertained that Father Thomas's eyes were firmly shut, then quickly dunked two fingers into the porridge and scooped it into his mouth. He had barely tasted the sticky food when a firm blow on the back of his head sent his hands flying into his bowl.

"There will be no eating when Father Thomas is talking to our Lord," hissed Mister Hall, his bald head red with outrage and orange hairs bristling from his ears. Mister Hall's angry outburst was over as quickly as it had come and Father Thomas continued with his prayer.

"Thank you, Lord, for all the gifts you have bestowed on us today. Thank you for providing these lost children with this home and thank you for giving me, and all the staff here, another day to minister to their souls. And for what we are about to receive ... make us truly grateful."

The chorus of *Aaah-men* was barely out of the mouths of the children before they were shovelling down spoonfuls of porridge. Red Wolf stared around him in disbelief, absently licking the sticky mess from his fingers.

It was now Mother Hall who whacked him on the back of his head. "Spoon!" she said, pushing a cold, shiny utensil into his hand. "Only savages eat with their hands."

Red Wolf took the spoon and copied the others, but he had lost his appetite and he did not like the taste of the food. He listened to the clanking and scraping of metal spoons on enamelled bowls. The sound was abrasive and jarring compared to the duller sound of maple ladles on maple bowls. He laid down his spoon and waited.

"*Nishin!* Eat. Quick," the boy next to him whispered in the language of The People. "If you don't, they hold you and push it down your throat. And you get a haircut like Henry over there!" He gestured with his lower lip to a boy who had a three-finger-wide strip of baldness running down the centre of his scalp from forehead to nape. In horror, Red Wolf ate the food, almost gagging on the lumps. He had barely finished when the bell clanged again and without a word the boys were instantly on their feet, waiting in silence in one of several lines to wash, dry, and stack their own dishes and spoons.

With the dishwashing done, and with the bell clanging yet again, the boys walked silently away in different directions.

Red Wolf didn't know where to go.

"Follow Henry," the other boy whispered. "He's in Grade One. He should be in Grade Two, like me, but he's doing Grade One again."

"Why?" Red Wolf asked.

"Because he's a stupid Indian."

CHAPTER SIX

Henry was easy to follow. His bald stripe set him apart, and once inside the Grade One classroom he was a head taller than the other boys. The teacher took Red Wolf's hand and led him to the front of the class. All the boys stared at the newcomer with expressionless faces, everyone except Henry, who sat front and centre with a scowl on his face.

"Say, 'Good morning' to George," the teacher instructed the class.

"Good morning to George," they said in unison.

Henry rolled his eyes at their stupidity.

Turning to face Red Wolf, the man pointed at his own chest. "Master Evans," he said, several times over until Red Wolf was able to repeat the name perfectly. This pleased the man, who smiled and tousled the boy's hair for a long time. Red Wolf felt uncomfortable.

Master Evans showed Red Wolf a nametag that said GEORGE. All of the children, except Henry, had similar nametags pinned to their shirts. When

Red Wolf successfully sounded out each letter of his new name, the teacher beamed and pinned the nametag on him. Then he pointed at Henry. "Henry, you may go back to your old desk now."

The big boy moved quickly to the back row, obviously happy to be returning to his old location. The teacher steered Red Wolf by his shoulders to the empty desk.

"Sit down!"

Red Wolf understood! He slid across the smooth oak seat that was still warm from Henry's backside. He wriggled around, slipping and sliding on the well-worn surface.

Suddenly a ruler smacked down on Red Wolf's desk a fraction of an inch from his arm. He jumped and let out a startled yelp, inadvertently banging his knees on the underside of the desk.

"Sit still!"

Red Wolf understood that, too.

Some of the boys were giggling, almost inaudibly, but Henry's laughter was loud and scornful.

Master Evans' voice was shrill. "Silence!"

The boys were quiet, and Red Wolf learned another word.

The teacher turned his back to the children and with a short white stick made marks on a large blackboard that hung on the wall. Red Wolf knew these must be the tracks his father had spoken of, the white man's signs that he must learn before he could leave school. He gazed at the marks and hoped for understanding. It didn't come.

The children lifted the tops of their desks, took out slates, and worked at copying the teacher's writing, their faces furrowed with concentration. Red Wolf did the same. He clutched the smooth stick in his fingers, chewed on his lower lip, and contemplated how to start. He made his first mark. The chalk screeched and snapped in two. Red Wolf was mortified. The teacher directed a chain of meaningless words at him, and he felt everyone's eyes boring into his back. He wished he could disappear. He closed his eyes tight, but when he reopened them he was still in the classroom, still at Bruce County Indian Residential School, still far from his parents and Crooked Ear. He picked up half of the chalk and made the same tapping sound as the other boys.

Master Evans was small-boned, almost to the point of being fragile. He was nothing like Mister Hall in size or weight. His voice was small, too, and he carried only a ruler, not a cane or strips of leather. Even so, when he walked up and down between the rows of desks, Red Wolf was afraid, and as his footsteps got closer Red Wolf tensed in anticipation of punishment. He knew that the marks he was making on the slate bore no similarity to those on the blackboard, just as the tracks made by Crooked Ear's paws were different from those made by the split hooves of a deer. By the time the teacher peered over his shoulder, sweat from the palms of his hands had dampened his slate.

Master Evans unclipped a thick wad of felt from his belt and leaned over.

Red Wolf flinched.

Master Evans wiped the slate clean. "Try again," he said.

Red Wolf breathed a sigh of relief.

In the way of The People, HeWhoWhistles had taught his son to observe; to watch and listen. Red Wolf was only five but he could identify a bird from its song. He could recognize the thumping hind feet of an alarmed rabbit, the huffing of rutting elk, the bark of a vixen calling her mate, the caw of a raven when food was close. He could even gauge approaching weather by listening to the wind and feeling it on his skin. So in the confines of the school where language gave him little informa-tion, he watched how hands moved and how facial expressions changed. He listened to tone of voice and inflection, unconsciously knowing that these things gave meaning to unfamiliar words.

It didn't take Red Wolf long to realize that Master Evans's voice rose in pitch just before he expected an answer. In response to that higher pitch, some boys threw one arm into the air and spoke in the foreign language. The master smiled and stroked their hair and spoke words that sounded happy. Red Wolf didn't have any answers in the new language and decided that silence would be the best way to stay out of trouble. When the teacher spoke directly to him, Red Wolf looked at his desk and anxiously fingered the scratched surface, worrying at a splinter until it broke free from the gouged wood. The teacher's sudden grip on his arm surprised and hurt him. The boy jumped to his feet, words of The People flying from his mouth, before he could capture them. "Ouch! That hurts. Let me go!"

The man wrestled him to the corner of the room and pushed him onto his knees facing the wall. Red Wolf stifled a yelp as the ruler slapped across his buttocks. He heard Henry snickering. Red Wolf was grateful, at least, for one thing: he was facing the wall, so no one could see him crying. But when tears escaped onto his cheek and he dabbed at them with his hand, Henry's snickers turned to full-blown laughter.

"Henry! Stop laughing," Master Evans ordered.

Red Wolf learned another phrase.

He felt as though a long, long time passed. He looked up to see the round face of a ticking machine that hung on the wall. He had no knowledge that it marked the passage of time, but he watched the pointers move. The one that made the ticking noise advanced around the circle more quickly than the other. When both pointed straight up, the school bell clanged again and the children got up from their seats.

"Stand up, George," Master Evans said. Red Wolf tried to stand and was aghast. His left leg was missing! He looked down expecting it not to be there. It was, but it wouldn't move and it felt heavy like a stone. He hopped on his right leg, dragging the useless leg behind him.

"It's gone numb from kneeling," Master Evans said, seeing the dismayed expression on Red Wolf's face. "It will be fine soon. Don't worry." The advice didn't help Red Wolf since he didn't understand, but the circulation soon returned, bringing with it an unpleasant tingling.

He hobbled after the others, along the corridor toward the refectory. Henry turned and waited for him to catch up. Red Wolf limped toward him, watching the expression on his face. By the time he was close enough to read malevolence in Henry's eyes it was too late. Henry's fist sank into his gut, doubling him over and forcing him backwards with a grunt. He staggered and fell to the floor.

"Henry!" Master Evans shouted. "Come with me to my office!"

Henry threw a disdainful glance at Red Wolf then walked away with Master Evans.

In the refectory, Turtle, the boy who had spoken to Red Wolf at breakfast, beckoned him with a subtle movement of his chin. After the encounter with Henry, Red Wolf wondered if he should ignore the gesture, but he read no malice or contradiction in Turtle's face, only open friendship. Turtle slid along the bench enough for Red Wolf to squeeze in. The two boys didn't speak, but the closeness made Red Wolf melt inside. He almost cried.

The midday meal was stew. It was not as good as his mother's. It didn't smell or taste smoky the way food should, but the chunks of potato and ragged cubes of fatty meat warmed his stomach. Apart from the slurping and scraping of spoons, there was silence. Red Wolf wiped his bowl clean with a hunk of bread, hoping there would be more, but there wasn't. He was pleased at least that his dish was so clean it didn't need washing. Nevertheless, he had to wait in line to go through the ritual.

After dishwashing, Turtle pushed his chin toward the growing line of Grade One children, and Red Wolf understood that he was to line up there. He flashed a smile of gratitude to Turtle, but the boy was already hurrying away. Red Wolf glanced around for Henry and was relieved when he realized that, as yet anyway, the older boy was nowhere to be seen. Red Wolf followed the Grade

Ones to the back of the building, where work clothes hung on numbered pegs. Like a swarm of bees swooping into flowers, the boys homed in on their own pegs. Red Wolf looked at the washed-out numbers on his hand and tried to find a peg number that looked the same. Panic was rising in his throat by the time he spotted it. The same number was stitched across the back of the tan coverall that hung on the peg, as well as on the chest pocket. *So they know it's me from the front as well as the back*, he thought. The boots that stood as a neat pair under the peg were numbered, too. They had mud on the soles and were creased to the shape of another boy's foot. Red Wolf wondered if the boy who had worn them had gone home. He hoped so.

He watched other children untie their school boots by pulling on the free end of a lace. He yanked at his own lace and was relieved when the bow unravelled. He plunged his feet into the work boots. They were much too big, but at least he could wiggle his toes. He tried to lace them, but the process for tying was much more complicated than untying. A man was bearing down on him, a cane tapping the floor. Red Wolf froze like a frightened fawn, hoping the predator would pass him by. But the man stopped. Red Wolf crunched down, hands covering his head, waiting for the cane to strike.

"Watch," the man said, squatting and tying the lace slowly so that Red Wolf could see. "Now you try."

After two attempts Red Wolf was wearing a pair of laced-up work boots. His feet slipped and slid inside them as he clomped after the other children through the back door of the school to the farm. The autumn sun shone from a clear blue sky and the air was fresh and clean, but Red Wolf didn't notice. He was completely absorbed, watching the man's cane rap the legs of boys who strayed marginally from the rigid procession. Red Wolf felt the twinge of anticipation that his legs would be the next to be rapped. No one spoke except for the man. He barked incomprehensible orders, sending boys to different areas of the farm. Finally Red Wolf alone remained.

"I'm the farm manager," the man said in English. "They call me Mister Boss. Here we teach you how to grow food so you won't go hungry again." Ironically, Red Wolf's stomach grumbled its half-empty complaint. "The wandering lifestyle you all have, picking berries and hunting, isn't civilized. When the hunting is poor, especially in the winter, you go hungry, or even starve! Here you'll learn how to grow crops and how to raise animals for food."

He pointed to a red cow contained in a pen. The animal knelt and stretched her neck under the split rail fence, her nose pushing aside the purple asters until her long pink tongue could wrap around a clump of orchard grass. Then she staggered to her feet with her prize. Red Wolf heard the grass fibres tear and watched the cow's jaws grind slowly back and forth. For a few seconds he felt at peace.

The strike to his leg was light. It barely hurt at all, but it surprised him enough to make him yelp.

"Pay attention when I speak," the man ordered, shaking his cane at Red Wolf, "and come with me."

He guided Red Wolf to an area of weedy pasture.

"Here's the new worker," he said to a brown-skinned youth who was shouting commands at younger children. "Looks like you need him. I want all this dug by the end of the week. Think you can do that?"

"Yes, sir, Mister Boss," said the youth, handing Red Wolf a shovel.

"I'll leave you in charge then," the man said as he walked away.

Once the boss was out of earshot, the youth spoke, but in yet another language that Red Wolf did not understand! Red Wolf remained silent, and the youth tried again.

"*Anishnaabe?*"

Red Wolf nodded. The youth smiled and continued in a mix of English and signs that the child understood "Me no speak *Anishnaabemowen*. Me Mohawk. Me name Sparrow Hawk. They call me Frank, Top Boy Frank."

He spread his arms to indicate all the boys working in the field. "We many people; Cree, Anishnaabe, Huron, Métis, Mohawk. We speak many tongues. No understand each other. All must speak English."

"English," Red Wolf said, pronouncing the word perfectly.

Top Boy Frank smiled. "Good!" He placed his foot on the top edge of the shovel blade and pushed down with his body weight. "Dig," he said, "like this." His shovel cut through the turf and he deftly flipped it so the weeds and grass disappeared under the fresh brown earth. Red Wolf tried but lacked the strength and technique to cut through the thatch of vegetation. "You'll soon get it," Top Boy Frank encouraged. "Keep trying."

Red Wolf tried and tried. It was hard work and soon he flopped to the ground, exhausted.

"Get up!" Frank urged, pulling him up with one hand. "If Mister Boss sees you idling, I'll be in trouble as well as you." He pushed Red Wolf's shovel securely into the soil and propped the child against it. "Lean on your shovel, like this … and look like you're working."

In this position, Red Wolf watched a robin. The bird landed on the freshly turned soil and within a second of cocking its head sideways pounced on the exposed tail of a worm. The robin planted its feet firmly and tugged with all its might. The worm stretched, becoming narrower and paler, until it suddenly broke into two. The piece in the earth quickly wriggled back under the soil, but the piece in the robin's beak was promptly dispatched down the bird's gullet. The day before, when Red Wolf was still a child, he would have giggled, but today there was no laughter in him.

On the neighbouring farm an old man walked behind a plough. The workhorse knew the routine and plodded faithfully along the edge of the furrow, throwing her weight into the collar. The farmer's arthritic hands gripped the plough handles to stop the share from bucking. It was hard work for a man his age, but when he finished the field and was finally able to take his eyes away from the soil, he shook his head and sighed. In the distance small boys were ploughing a field with shovels.

CHAPTER SEVEN

Henry stormed across the field to join the diggers. Red Wolf wasn't the only one who watched him approach. Several other Grade One boys monitored his progress, and Top Boy Frank watched, too.

"Did Master Evans keep you back after class again?" Frank asked quietly.

Henry didn't reply. Instead he shoved Red Wolf on both shoulders. "It was your fault," he yelled.

Red Wolf felt tears welling up, but he gulped down the sob that tried to burst from his chest.

Henry drew close, carefully forming his words and spitting them into Red Wolf's ear. "Next time, don't make a sound, you hear! And don't tell anyone, or else...." He leered and drew his index finger across Red Wolf's neck. The child didn't need to know the language to understand the threat. His knees buckled.

"That's enough, Henry," Frank said, sheltering Red Wolf with his body. "Leave him alone. Don't make me report you again. Get to work."

Henry snatched up a shovel and started attacking the soil. Red Wolf was shocked to see that Frank watched Henry with compassion! Red Wolf didn't understand why. He hated Henry!

A warning whistle, not unlike a jay's strident call, pierced the air and all the boys in the old pasture began digging with renewed vigour. Someone was coming: a man and a dog. Red Wolf looked up and his heart leapt into his throat. It was the man called Indian agent.

It all seemed so long ago now when the white man had ridden into the summer camp of The People. That was the day it had all started, he thought, the day the man had invaded his childhood and had called him Horse Thief. He was no longer the carefree boy who had walked with the chestnut gelding that sunny afternoon, just a few moons ago. Since then he had lost everything.

He threw his weight behind the shovel and averted his head, hoping the white man would not recognize him, but the hound ambled straight toward him, tail wagging gently, a happy greeting on his face.

"Get over here, dog!" the Indian agent yelled. The animal lowered his head, rounded his back, and with tail between his legs approached his master. He was rewarded for his obedience with a raised hand and a harsh voice. "Don't you be getting friendly with the Indians."

The dog sighed and flopped to the ground.

"I hear that my special friend is here at last," the man called out to no one in particular. Red Wolf froze like a frightened rabbit. "Ah, there he is!"

The Indian agent loosely wrapped a meaty arm around Red Wolf's neck and rubbed his head in an amicable manner. Fear paralyzed the child. The man's powerful bicep tightened against his throat.

"Horse Thief!" he whispered, his breath rank against Red Wolf's cheek. "I said we would meet again, did I not?"

Red Wolf could barely breathe, and the Algonquian words stabbed at his heart like a hunting knife.

Then, as suddenly as it had started, it was over. The man released him, turned on his heels, and walked away. "Dog!" he yelled.

Red Wolf gasped and realized that he was trembling.

The dog dragged himself up and slunk after his owner.

As the sun changed its angle in the sky, Red Wolf's hands started to blister and then the blisters broke and oozed.

"You'd better go to the infirmary," Top Boy Frank said.

"Firmamy?" Red Wolf questioned.

A voice spoke in the language of The People. "I'll take you."

Red Wolf looked around and smiled at Turtle, following him to the school building.

A young woman in a white apron greeted the boys. "Hello," she said, her voice light and warm. "What can I do for you?"

Turtle held up Red Wolf's hands. The nurse made sympathetic noises and turned to get cotton and alcohol to clean the wounds. "What have you been doing?" she asked.

"Digging the old pasture," Turtle replied.

"That's a man's job," she said, shaking her head. "This will hurt a bit, I'm afraid."

Red Wolf winced and tried to pull his hand away, but she held it firmly. "We have to make sure it's clean."

She turned to Turtle. "Bring a biscuit for the wounded farmer and take one for yourself."

Before the boys had taken more than one bite, brisk footsteps were heard echoing down the corridor, getting louder and closer.

"Swallow fast," whispered the nurse.

Mother Hall appeared at the door just as the boys gulped down the biscuits. Her small, critical eyes appraised both boys before settling on Turtle. "There's nothing wrong with you, boy. Get back to work."

Turtle silently obeyed.

She then examined Red Wolf's palms. "Why are you here, wasting time for just a few blisters? Outside! Go!"

"I'd like him to stay another moment while I bandage his hands," the nurse said.

"Bandages!" Mother Hall shrieked. "We can't be wasting good bandages on such trivial things. He needs to get back out there and start toughening up those hands. Work will harden them in no time."

She grabbed Red Wolf by the scruff of his cover-all and lifted him to the tips of his big leather boots. With years of experience behind her, she steered him out of the doorway into the corridor, releasing him with a firm shove. Red Wolf stumbled away from her as fast as he could but stopped dead in his tracks when her high-pitched voice shrieked what he now understood was his new name.

"Three-six-six," she yelled, reading the number on the back of his coverall and pointing to the wooden floor. "Look at this mess! Get back here and clean it up."

Red Wolf looked where she pointed and saw fresh earth that had fallen from his boots.

"We don't wear farm boots in school," Mother Hall ordered, rolling her eyes. "Take them off immediately."

The nurse stood behind Mother Hall and mimed taking off boots. Red Wolf sat on the floor and tried to yank the uncomfortable things from his feet, forgetting that first he had to untie the laces. Knowing that the rawhide strips would soon be whizzing through the air and cutting painfully into some part of his body, he tugged at the laces, but his palms were slippery with sweat, and salt was stinging the raw flesh.

Mother Hall turned to the nurse. "Oh, Lord. He still don't know how to untie his laces!"

"Don't worry, Mother Hall, I'll help him with his boots," the nurse said, squatting beside Red Wolf and unravelling the bows. "Then I'll make sure he sweeps the floor."

"Humph!" Mother Hall turned her attention back to the infirmary. "Who's this?" she asked, looking at a gaunt child who lay motionless under clean white sheets.

"Three-five-nine," the nurse answered.

Mother Hall shook the boy, but there was no response. "What's wrong with him?"

"He's not eating or drinking," the nurse said, "but the wire snags look clean, they're not infected."

Comprehension lit the older woman's eyes. "Wire snags! He's the boy who tried to climb the fence?"

"Yes. He got hooked on the barbed wire."

"He's malingering, using the caning as an excuse to get out of work."

The nurse sighed. "I don't think so. In my opinion he's homesick and heartsick."

"That's nonsense!" the housemother said. "Indians don't have emotions like we do. He's just shirking. If he's not eating and drinking, force-feed him!"

Red Wolf's first day finally drew to a close. His legs were wobbly with fatigue. He wanted to clamber into bed fully clothed, but the fear of punishment forced him to stay upright long enough to change into his nightgown. However, by the time the boys chanted *Now I lay me down to sleep*, Red Wolf was dead to the world.

Mother Hall watched him. He lay on his back, his chest rising and falling under the blanket. She knew she should wake him and make him kneel at the side of his bed to recite the prayer. Father Thomas would expect that of her. But she looked at the child's relaxed face and felt a tug of sympathy. She decided that prayers weren't that important anyway. At least the boy had folded his clothes and put them away before falling asleep.

Red Wolf walked on the beach at Clear Lake, where he had grown up. Darkness was falling, but he could still make out the bluffs and trees that sheltered the

beach from the strong north wind, and he could see the ridge where the wolves sometimes howled. He snuggled between his grandfather and his grandmother, their furs draped over his shoulders, his sleepy eyes watching the orange-blue tongues of fire lick the embers. HeWhoWhistles and the other hunters sat around the big drum. With powerful forearms the men pounded their sticks against the skin, their high-pitched voices throbbing in time with the rhythm.

The women danced around the men in a circle, the old ones shuffling in the gravelly sand, the younger ones pointing their toes and lifting their feet in time to the strong heartbeat of the drum. StarWoman laughed and copied her younger sister, who had broken loose with a spinning dance that took her on a path outside the circle of more stately women.

Suddenly HeWhoWhistles' piercing voice soared above the drumbeat. StarWoman danced over to her husband and stood behind him, lending her support and spiritual power to his voice. This was the way of The People, and Red Wolf knew that it was his way too. HeWhoWhistles' song gave thanks to Creator and to the four-legged that had given their lives in order that the lives of The People would be sustained. He gave thanks to Mother Earth for providing yet again, enabling them to survive another long hard winter, and for the upcoming bounty of summer that would allow them to refill their baskets and prepare for another season of hardship. This, too, was the Anishnaabe *way*.

Red Wolf followed the bright sparks that rode a distance on the wind. He felt something warm inside his chest. It wasn't just the fire, or the furs. He glanced up at the ridge and saw them! The wolves! He listened to their howl and his heart was filled with joy.

A bell clanged and Red Wolf knew something was wrong. Bells did not ring on the beach at Clear Lake. He looked at the sparks from the fire and watched them get snuffed into blackness.

He awoke. He could have wept.

CHAPTER EIGHT

Other than a word here or there, the only time that Red Wolf and Turtle could talk was when they were both assigned to Frank's work crew. Whenever the farm manager was out of earshot, Top Boy Frank ignored the rule of silence. Even so, Turtle was cautious. He was a year older than Red Wolf and knew that having friends was not allowed, that they would be punished and separated. But between furtive glances he answered Red Wolf's questions and explained the meaning of words and phrases. He taught Red Wolf how to lower his eyes and say with the right degree of contriteness, "I sorry, mother, I bad Indian." Or "Please forgive filthy savage."

Sometimes these supplications averted a caning.

At first the two boys communicated in the language of The People, then a mix of English and *Anishnaabemowin*, until, finally, they spoke mostly in English. But questions arose in Red Wolf's mind that he couldn't ask his friend in either language;

questions that were too difficult to speak aloud, such as why his parents had left him at the school, why they didn't come to take him home, why they didn't want him anymore. He wondered if it was because he was a *dirty savage* and a *good-for-nothing Indian*.

Red Wolf thought about the wrinkle-faced infant who had arrived in the *wiigwam* just before the family had moved to the reserve, just before his father had left him here at the school. The baby had demanded so much of his mother's time, and he remembered being mad at both StarWoman and the noisy baby, because they were so engrossed by one another. He wondered if his mother had sent him away because he was angry, or because she loved the new baby more than him. He kept these thoughts to himself.

But one afternoon when the two boys were bagging corn cobs, one of Red Wolf's unspeakable questions came flying out of his mouth, unbidden.

"Do you ever stop missing your mother and father?"

Turtle sighed. "No!"

A sob heaved from Red Wolf's chest. He couldn't contain it. Brimming tears stung his eyes and he thought his heart was breaking.

Turtle's voice quivered. "My sister is here, too."

Red Wolf pushed his knuckles into his eyelids, forcing back the tide of tears. "Girls? Here? Where?" he said, smearing dirt over his contorted face.

"On the other side."

Red Wolf frowned.

"Don't you know?" Turtle continued. "There's a line right through the middle of the school. Upstairs it's a wall, but downstairs it's a door, just past Father Thomas's office. The girls stay on one side and the boys stay on the other."

Red Wolf was disbelieving. "I've never seen any girls! Where are they now? Don't they have to work?"

"They don't work on the farm. They work in the laundry."

Red Wolf's brow furrowed.

"Mother Hall doesn't wash our sheets and clothes. The girls do," Turtle said.

"Where do they eat?" Red Wolf asked, wondering how he had lived in the building for all these weeks without seeing a single girl.

"I don't know," Turtle said.

"But if your sister is here, why can't you see her?"

"They won't let me!"

Red Wolf was perplexed. "But —"

Turtle raised his voice. "I don't know why not! They just won't let me! But I'm going over to the other side one day. I'll find her. I don't care what they do to me."

Red Wolf continued bagging cobs in silence. "Do we ever get to eat any of this?" he eventually asked.

"No! It goes to a place called Market. The teachers get some, I think, but not us." Checking on the whereabouts of the farm manager, Turtle peeled back the green leaves from an ear of corn and sank his teeth into the yellow cob. "You take what you can, when you can." A kernel flew from his mouth along with the words.

Red Wolf followed Turtle's example and chomped into a cob, the raw kernels tasting sweet and starchy. Suddenly another question came unbidden. "What does *savage* mean?"

Turtle didn't reply until he had nibbled every trace of yellow from the cob and was busy picking corn from his teeth. "It's what we are," he said.

Someone sounded a warning, a good imitation of a jay's call. The Indian agent and his dog were walking across the field. The two boys pushed the gnawed cobs deep into the sacks and headed toward the wagon.

The dog once again sought out Red Wolf. The child smiled as he stroked the soft brown coat, unfortunately exposing a telltale piece of yellow corn still caught between his front teeth.

"Horse Thief!" shouted the Indian agent, grabbing Red Wolf's jaw and parting his lips to reveal the evidence. "Or should I say Corn Thief. Once a thief, always a thief, is what I say. Here's the lesson I promised you about property; everything is ours and nothing is yours! You own nothing, you have nothing, you *are* nothing! Understand? I tried to warn you, I tried to spare you the pain of punishment, but I see that you didn't heed my friendly advice. That was a mistake, boy. And now you've exhausted my generosity and my goodwill. Mister Hall has a special place to put bad boys like you. Let's go."

Red Wolf curled up and watched the sky through the narrow cracks between the rough-sawn boards. *The Crate* was aptly named, having started life as a packing crate. Twenty years earlier, it had brought all of Mother Hall's worldly possessions across the sea from England; her bed linens and clothes, some dishes, pans, and trinkets. There was barely enough space for a small boy to turn around, and if he had stood upright he would have hit his head on the ceiling. Everything in his body yelled *move, run, get away, be free*. But he was trapped like an animal in a cage.

Even more than the ache in his cramped limbs, Red Wolf ached for his mother. Tears came just at the thought of her. He rocked back and forth, clutching his knees to his chest, convulsive sobs heaving from his chest. He was totally alone, utterly abandoned. Someone pushed a cup of water and a chunk of bread through a small flap. A boy whispered. Red Wolf stopped crying and listened. He didn't understand the words, but the voice was kind and Red Wolf thought that the boy was saying something encouraging.

"Stay with me, please," Red Wolf begged in *Anishnaabemowin*, his voice small and faltering, but the boy went away and Red Wolf was alone again. He held the bread on his lap but couldn't eat. He wasn't hungry.

He closed his eyes and dozed. The line between memory and dream faded, taking him back to the summer camp of The People. HeWhoWhistles was teaching him, finding lessons in the most unlikely places.

"Look well, and the story will tell itself," he advised, studying two pairs of entangled antlers that pointed skyward. "Two moose fought here for the right to father the next generation. Their antlers became entangled and one of them died from a broken neck. See? The other could have died slowly from thirst. But I think not. Look at Crooked Ear."

The young wolf was whining softly while snuffling his nose deep into the ground.

"I think that wolves found this trapped moose and they ended his life swiftly. Crooked Ear can smell them! Perhaps they were part of his family.

"And look at these tiny teeth marks on the bones! A mouse has gnawed here. The strong bones of the moose have passed even into the frail body of a mouse! The mouse will be eaten by an owl or a hawk or maybe even a wolf. And eventually the bleached bones that remain here will become part of the earth, enriching it and allowing it to grow grass that another generation of grazing animals. Everything in death returns to give life to others. A bird has even made a nest here in the crook of the antlers."

Half asleep and half awake, Red Wolf watched strands of hair unravel from the abandoned nest and flutter in the breeze. The hair was long and dark like his mother's. He wondered if it had been hers.

He opened his eyes and the crate closed in on him again. He was a prisoner. Fresh tears stung his sore eyes. He wondered if Crooked Ear had indeed been able to smell his family in the soil around the moose antlers. He hoped so. He wished that he had something to snuffle, something that would give him the faintest trace of his mother. He had nothing.

The light started to fade and a deer mouse darted through a gap between the boards. It paused, sat back on its haunches, and raised one dainty forepaw. Its delicate ears trembled and its long whiskers twitched, as though it was weighing the scent of danger against the aroma of food. Red Wolf breathed softly. The mouse scurried over his boot and up his leg. It gnawed anxiously at the crust of bread. Red Wolf longed to touch it, to stroke its velvety coat, to feel its warmth, but when he gingerly stretched out a hand, the mouse scampered away.

Reaching inside his coverall and deep into his trouser pocket, his fingers rubbed the wolf pendant. In a moment of inspiration he took the lace from his left boot, threaded it through the hole in the pendant and tied it around his neck. With the pendant tucked carefully inside his clothing and nestled against his chest, he felt better. Silently he prayed, *Brother wolf, help me get away from here.* But his prayer was answered by feelings of home that were almost too much for him to bear.

As darkness fell, cold seeped into his bones. He tucked himself into a ball, warming his hands under his armpits. Far off in the distance he heard the lonely howl of a wolf. He threw back his head and, as loud as he dared, howled a reply.

CHAPTER NINE

By the end of the first term Red Wolf had made a transition in language. Instead of translating English to *Anishnaabemowin* in his head, he now thought in English. He was stunned when he woke up one morning and realized that his dream had even been in English. He understood most of the instructions he was given throughout the day and many of the words in the lessons, although the concepts were confusing, especially in the religious studies classes. And due to the code of silence that was enforced for so much of the day, he had limited his opportunity to practice speaking the new language.

It was a school tradition that the Grade One class performed the pageant on Christmas Eve. Red Wolf didn't understand what it was all about. Weeks ahead of time, Master Evans picked children to play the different roles. He chose the smallest boy in the class to be Mary. The boy was dressed in a blue robe and wore a sheet draped over his head, tied with a cord so it flowed over his shoulders and back. Master Evans announced that the biggest boy in the class would play the part of Joseph, but then changed his mind when he realized that Henry was the biggest boy. He gave the Joseph costume to the second biggest boy instead. Henry was not in the play, at least not dressed up as an actor. He had a special job as Master Evans' assistant, working *behind the scenes*.

The three *best* boys in the class were selected as wise men. Their outfits were colourful and grand, with trailing cloaks, sparkling necklaces, and shiny crowns covered in glass beads. Red Wolf wished he were a wise man. He couldn't stop wondering what *gifts* were inside the carved wooden boxes they carried. His own robe was simple and dull, coarse and itchy, and loosely tied at the waist with twine, but his headband reminded him of those worn by The People, and he went barefoot! It felt nice compared to the school uniform.

On the evening of the big show the children went to the barn. A silver star had been hung from the roof on a long piece of wire, and it glittered in the light from the lanterns. One of the cow stalls had been thoroughly cleaned and fresh straw strewn over the stone floor. A feed trough, so new you could smell the pine, was positioned in the middle of the stall, and a white baby doll, wrapped in a shawl, lay in the trough on an overflowing bed of hay.

The curious cows in the neighbouring stalls poked their heads over the dividing wall. Red Wolf was mesmerized. One, called Jersey, had a coat the colour of the forest floor in autumn, big brown eyes, large furry ears, and a wet black nose. She reminded Red Wolf of a deer. He stifled a laugh when her long pink tongue reached out to lick her own nostrils. Red Wolf stuck out his own tongue and stretched it upward. It didn't go as far as his nose.

One grade at a time, the children came to the barn to see the show. Mary, in the blue robe, sat on a stool behind the feed trough and obeyed Master Evans' directions to look down *lovingly* at the doll in the hay. Joseph stood next to the boy in blue and *gently* rested a hand on his shoulder. In response to Master Evans' cue, Red Wolf led the shepherds *excitedly* down the barn aisle and through the open door of the stall. They each knelt at the feed trough and peered *adoringly* into the face of the doll, then regrouped on the right side of Joseph. Finally, the three wise men marched *regally* down the barn aisle and bowed *respectfully* in front of the feed trough. They put their gifts *worshipfully* on the ground, then stood on the left side of Joseph in what Master Evans called a balanced stage.

The actors then stood *quietly* while all of the children in the grade had the opportunity to look through the stall door at the scene, or peer over the wall if they were tall enough. Red Wolf felt uncomfortable with everyone staring at him. Then everyone sang the song that the entire school had spent weeks learning.

Away in a manger no crib for a bed

The little Lord Jesus laid down his sweet head.

The stars in the bright sky looked down where he lay

(The silver star twinkled and twirled in the moving air ... right over the feed trough.)

The little Lord Jesus asleep in the hay.

The cattle are lowing

(The cows mooed, as if on cue.)

The baby awakes, but little Lord Jesus no crying he makes.

(The boy in the blue robe picked up the doll and rocked it in his arms.)

I love Thee, Lord Jesus, look down from the sky

(The shepherds and wise men stared at the doll with smiles pasted on their faces.)

And stay by my side, until morning is nigh.

At the end of the song, Father Thomas beamed and the teacher ushered his class back to the school building, humming as he went. The wise men picked up their gift boxes and retreated to the far end of the barn, followed by the shepherds, where they all awaited the arrival of the next grade.

It wasn't until the following Christmas, when Red Wolf watched other Grade Ones perform the identical pageant, that he realized "Mary" was a girl's name, that the boy in blue was supposed to be the mother of Jesus, and the boxes that the wise men carried were empty.

CHAPTER TEN

After the small Upright had disappeared into the waves of sun-bleached grass, Crooked Ear had waited in the shelter of the forest for the child to return, but the tall Upright had come back alone. The days were becoming shorter and instinct was tugging at his paws, telling them to go back to the place of his birth, back to the granite ridge at Clear Lake. But there was a stronger force tugging at him, also, and he followed it ... right to the barbed-wire fence of the school. Under the cover of darkness he trotted around the perimeter, looking for a way past the fence, but there was none. He stood on his hind legs and stretched his forelegs as far as they would go, feeling the sharp barbs of the wire. He whined softly and scrabbled at the base of the fence, but the wire went into the earth also. He could smell his little Upright, but there were many other smells too, ones that filled him with fear. He spun, broke into a lope, and started the journey back to Clear Lake.

Snow was falling long before Crooked Ear reached the place of his birth. He pushed on through the cold, his limbs cramping with exhaustion, his instinct telling him that respite was not far away. He loped the last few miles and rushed into the old pack with tail wagging and a lupine smile across his face.

His mother and father and siblings were not there to greet him.

The pack stared at him with an aloofness that bordered on hostility. Crooked Ear knew what to do. He lowered his head, tail, and ears. He averted his gaze from their amber and yellow eyes. He flattened his body toward the ground. He held this pose for a few seconds, his keen senses judging the reaction among the other wolves. One, alone, bared his fangs and snarled. Crooked Ear discerned that this wolf was the pack's new alpha male, and he recognized him: his Uncle Seraph, Tall-Legs's younger brother. The rest of the pack waited for Seraph to make the decision as to whether or not Crooked Ear would be allowed back into the family. In the silence Crooked Ear judged that things were not going well. He was about to roll onto his back in the ultimate gesture of submission when Seraph charged.

Crooked Ear stumbled as he veered away. It slowed him down. Seraph's jaws locked onto his throat, fangs pierced his flesh, body weight pinned him to the ground. Crooked Ear struggled briefly, but he was not yet fully grown. He lacked the muscle and body weight of his uncle, he was depleted from the exhausting journey, and he had not eaten for two days. Instinct told him to submit with what could be his last breath. He lay still.

As quickly as the attack started, it was over. Seraph released Crooked Ear and returned to the others. They crowded around him, backing him up, growling at the interloper, their lips withdrawn, their gleaming fangs exposed.

Crooked Ear dragged himself to his feet and slunk away. He slept alone in a shallow scrape under the cover of thick balsam branches. He curled up as tightly as he could, his chin resting on all four paws so his breath warmed them, his bushy tail encircling him. When snow fell it cloaked him, adding insulation and rendering him invisible. Even the tip of his nose was perfectly camouflaged among the dark balsam cones. A passerby would never have suspected he was there.

Crooked Ear's urge to be with the pack was, however, strong. He wanted to curl up and sleep next to other wolves, to feel their breath, to benefit from the warmth of the huddle. But more than that, he needed to be with the pack in order to find food to survive the winter. He quickly learned how close he could be without enraging Seraph. And for a while that was where he stayed, on the fringe, barely in sight of the other wolves. But as the nights became colder and food scarcer, he moved closer, submitting to Seraph many times a day. Gradually the alpha's anger was replaced by cool disregard and tolerance. This change permitted the others to accept Crooked Ear into the pack, as long as he stayed at the bottom of the hierarchy.

It was a hard, hungry winter, and all the wolves lost weight, but Crooked Ear, low in social standing, was particularly thin. His coat was lacklustre, and although the long guard hairs still disguised his ribs, little flesh covered his skeleton.

Finally the breeze blew soft, and once again the wolves stretched out on the great slabs of granite that angled slightly towards the sky. Beneath them, the glare ice of Clear Lake was criss-crossed with grey-brown fissures and gleaming channels of black water, but high on the ridge the rocks had been swept clean of snow by winter winds and warmed by the spring sunshine. It was here that they lay, just as their ancestors had for centuries.

Seraph was in a relaxed mood and Crooked Ear, taking advantage of his uncle's congeniality, flopped on his side with the other wolves, his thick winter coat absorbing the sun's rays. At one year, he was almost full grown. He was lofty, as his father had been, but still lacked the girth and muscle of a mature wolf.

Seraph raised his head and blinked his sleepy eyes then leapt to his feet, alert and attentive, stretching his head toward the scent carried on the breeze. With a whine and a wag of his bushy tail, he sprang off the rocks and trotted down the narrow trail that led to the trees. The other wolves stretched, yawned, and followed him to where the balsam firs grew dense and dark. There, on the south-facing slope, where the sun peeked through the trees, a pile of freshly excavated sandy soil marked the entrance to the old den where Seraph's mate had recently birthed their first litter.

The wolves cocked their heads in response to the mewling that came from deep underground. Seraph bowed down and rested his head on enormous paws, a whine of anticipation coming from his throat. In response, the she-wolf crawled along the root-lined tunnel into the daylight.

Seraph bounded toward her but stopped abruptly when he saw the angle of her ears and the stony stare in her yellow eyes. Tentatively he sniffed the air, savouring the unfamiliar smells of birth and milk that mingled with the alluring odour of she-wolf. He stretched toward her, but her withdrawn lips told him that she was in no mood to be friendly. He took a step back and observed with all of his senses. Her hairless belly was slung low with two rows of swollen teats, ribs stared out of her coarse coat, and hip bones protruded through the tight skin of her haunches. Seraph spun and loped down the well-worn trail, where thin soil barely covered the ancient rocks of the Canadian Shield. The other wolves scrambled after him, their claws gaining traction on the stubborn patches of packed, dirty snow. Survival of the offspring was now the pack's shared priority.

Crooked Ear was the first to return, a mouse held gently in his lips.

The den held strong memories of his own mother, memories he could not resist. He entered, dragging himself down the tunnel on his belly. Despite his offering, the she-wolf bared her fangs, snarling and growling viciously. He dropped the rodent and quickly retreated, rump first, into Seraph. Fortunately the alpha's fangs were clamped onto a vole and all he could do was lash out with his front claws. Crooked Ear veered away and retreated to the perimeter of the pack once more.

The she-wolf moved to the trees and urinated, then, flattening herself to the ground, she crawled back inside the den. The mewling intensified for a few moments as each of the squirrel-sized pups scrambled on wobbly legs to find a source of nourishment and comfort. Soon their crying was replaced by sucking, swallowing, and snuffled breathing.

Crooked Ear did his part in feeding the she-wolf, who, in turn, fed the growing pups. Of the five, four remained. The runt had been sickly from birth. During the first few hours she had vigorously licked the floppy creature and had repeatedly pushed it toward her belly, but it lacked the strength to nurse. She nosed it to one side of the den, away from the others. As soon as she realized that there was no breath coming from its nose, she licked it one last time, and then, in the manner of wolves, she ate it.

Even in their sleep, the wolves heard the far-off call of the ravens and knew that the big birds had spotted prey. Heads popped out from under bushy tails and ears pricked up, alert. Crooked Ear stood and shook the balsam needles from his coat, then, quivering with anticipation, he raised his voice in chorus with the pack. In the excitement, the wolves chased their own tails and nipped at each other until a stare from Seraph's yellow eyes silenced them. They followed him as he loped toward the voices of the ravens, leaving the new mother standing at the entrance to the den. She sighed and returned to her pups.

Crooked Ear watched the other wolves closely. They all took their orders from Seraph, a glare from his eyes rooting them to the spot or telling them to advance. The limited hunting that Crooked Ear had done with his parents had taught him little. Now he was learning that every member of the pack had a part to play in surrounding the prey, worrying it, and tiring it so that the kill could be made without injury to the wolf itself. He was learning patience, planning, and stealth. He was learning the way of the wolf.

They approached the elk from downwind, long strands of saliva drooling onto their paws. With bodies low to the ground, and moving so as not to snap a twig, they skirted the herd, fanning out, eyes and noses searching every detail. The cows were heavy with young. In a few weeks the new-borns would be easy targets, but the experienced wolves knew that right now the females would not go down easily. They would fight.

The elk sniffed the air, their senses attuned to any noise or smell that might indicate the presence of a predator. They gingerly inched away from the oval depressions in the snow where they had slept, away from the yellow, urine-stained craters, away from the safety of the cedar stand, out to where straw-coloured seed heads stood tall above a tangled thatch of winter-damaged grass. Some pawed the ground to remove snow from the matted pasture. Others wrapped their tongues around tall stems and chewed, their jaws moving from side to side in a fal-tering motion.

The wolves spotted an old bull, moving stiffly from one patch of snow-covered grass to another. Its ribs and haunches protruded through rough hair, its mane was matted, and its antlers, which would be formidable weapons later in the season, were harmless velvet-covered buds.

The wolves closed in. A cow, her nostrils twitching, caught the first scent of danger. She raised her tail, warning the others with the flash of white. Eyes wide with panic, the elk moved closer together. The wolves stood tall. Realizing they were surrounded on three sides by their most feared predator, the herd bolted for the only opening in sight. The wolves exploded toward the old bull, cutting it off from the panicked herd and driving it toward Seraph, who waited in the undergrowth. When the bull elk was almost upon him, Seraph leaped, sinking his fangs into its throat.

Crooked Ear joined the others, jumping onto its back and clinging with his teeth as the bull spun and bucked. Finally, another wolf grabbed the elk's muzzle, clamping down over its nose and mouth. Desperate to breathe, the elk thrashed its head from side to side, lifting the wolf from the ground and sweeping him back and forth, but the wolf held firm. With a thud that shook the earth, the old elk fell heavily on his side.

There was a brief moment of silence.

Then powerful jaws crunched through bone and flesh.

Cloven hooves pawed the air.

Legs flailed in a desperate bid to run.

And life poured from the elk into the wolves.

Ravens watched from the trees as the wolves ripped into the soft underbelly of the old bull elk. Seraph turned on the others, growling ferociously, driving them back a few paces, where they snarled and squabbled among themselves. He pushed aside steaming intestines and tore the liver out of the body cavity. With two chomps of his massive teeth it was gone. Pushing his bloodied nose back into the tangle of guts, he rooted through to find the heart. Then, with a barely perceptible motion of his ears, he allowed the pack to join him.

The wolves snatched whatever was closest while trying to maintain their own pecking order. Crooked Ear was at the bottom. Even though he had played his part in bringing down the elk, he had to remain on the edge of the kill. Finally, as stomachs started to fill, Crooked Ear was allowed into the circle to feed.

Satisfied, with skin pulled taught across their distended bellies, the wolves ambled homeward, leaving the ravens tearing at the bulging intestines. A red vixen approached on silent pads. The ravens attacked and she retreated to wait her turn, along with those who had caught the scent on the wind and were still travelling toward the kill.

Within hours nothing would remain of the old elk except for a few fragments of bone and fur.

CHAPTER ELEVEN

Spring was on its way, yet winter was not willing to relinquish its hold. Despite the warmer temperatures that had melted all but the most obstinate patches of snow, the trees remained bare. Then, suddenly, violets wearing hats of dried leaves popped up from the forest floor and bronze beech leaves that had rasped on slim branches all winter long were pushed aside by the force of new buds. A green carpet rolled across the landscape from south to north and, almost overnight, the school lawn became verdant. Mother Hall's daffodils pierced the ground with their spear-like leaves and within days their yellow trumpets nodded in the sun.

It was a bright Thursday morning in May. Mother Hall entered the dormitory, her arms full of ironed shirts. This was unusual because the boys knew that Sunday was the day for clean clothes, not Thursday.

Cleanliness was next to godliness and both these things coincided with chapel on Sundays. Mother Hall seemed jittery, in fact, a bundle of nerves. Promising a whipping to any boy who got his shirt dirty, she announced that an important man would be visiting them in the classroom, so they would stay inside all day and had better be good, or else.

Around noon, a horse-drawn carriage rolled through the gates. Father Thomas greeted the visitor and escorted him to the staff dining room.

"I'd like you all to meet our school governor," he said to the assembled staff.

Mother Hall made a small curtsy. "It's so lovely to meet you, Governor," she said coyly in her most refined language. "You must be hungry after your long journey. We've prepared luncheon and the girls are waiting to serve, so please sit down."

The governor unbuttoned his coat and Mother Hall helped wrestle the sleeves from his arms. Father Thomas watched the guest settle his ample backside on the chair, and he sent up a silent prayer that the slender mahogany legs would withstand the weight.

"Grace!" he said in a rush, wanting to get through the meal before disaster struck. The boys bowed their heads and Father Thomas recited the shortest prayer he had ever uttered. "Heavenly Father, thank you for the food we are about to enjoy. Amen."

"We produce all our own food here, Governor," Mother Hall said as five schoolgirls, their brown hands covered in white gloves, served roast pork, squash, potatoes, and gravy.

"The children are surely spoiled by such abundance," the governor said, spreading his linen napkin over his rotund mid-section.

After several distracted bites and swallows, during which conversation was definitely not a priority, the governor directed his conversation to Father Thomas. "The board of governors is very pleased with the work that you are doing here, Father. I'm sure you'll agree with me that the residential school system is working wonderfully well. The government builds the schools and provides the funding, and you, at Bruce County, use that money to transform the children's lives. Obviously you do much more than just provide an education. You are civilizing the Indians, teaching them good behaviour, good manners, the difference between right and wrong."

He snapped his fingers at the closest serving girl and with his plate heaped for the second time, he continued. "Clearly, taking the children away from their families is a big help when it comes to assimilating them into our society, especially regarding Christianity. Separating them from their pagan communities gives us a far greater success rate, don't you agree?"

The governor didn't wait for a response. "We've been criticized for wasting money educating the females," he said, glancing at the serving girls, "but in my opinion, the fate of the next generation hangs on girls such as these! What will happen if the boys leave here and marry unschooled girls?"

The question was rhetorical, but Mother Hall valiantly tried to answer.

The governor ignored her, slapping his palms down on the table with a resounding smack that shook the water glasses. "They will fall back into their heathen ways! And the children from these marriages will almost certainly adopt the habits of their pagan mothers. All things considered, the money spent educating females is money well spent. By the next generation there won't be an Indian problem because the Indians will have been assimilated into our society."

"Yes, yes, quite so," Father Thomas agreed, anxious to steer the conversation to another topic. "But we do have a problem for next year, and I was hoping you might be able to help."

"That's what I'm here for, Father, but I'd like to talk more about —" The governor stopped in mid-sentence. Apple pie, piled high with dollops of fresh whipped cream, had appeared in front of him.

Father Thomas, seizing the opportunity of the governor's distraction, continued with his well-rehearsed speech. "Some of the children are now in Grade Eight, but we don't have the curriculum or the teachers for higher education. We have wonderful, dedicated people on staff here. They have a passion to bring the love of God to these children, but none of them are qualified in the field of education —"

The governor swallowed and intervened. "My good fellow, you don't understand —"

Father Thomas kept talking. "As you know, Governor, it's hard to find qualified educators willing to come out to these remote places and work with the Indians. I made an enormous sacrifice coming here, giving up a comfortable life in a well-to-do parish. But I have no regrets. This is my calling. Remuneration and worldly goods are of little importance compared to saving the souls of these boys and girls. I am, after all, storing up treasures in Heaven, not on earth, where moth and rust can destroy. It's what the Lord tells us to do."

One or two heads nodded in agreement.

"However, the problem is this — we need someone capable of teaching the older children. If we were to offer a more lucrative salary we could employ one or two trained teachers. So, in short, Governor, I need you to organize additional funding."

"My dear man," the governor said, wiping cream from his lips, "the policy of the government is to provide the children with an *elementary* education! We are not trying to turn out Indian students who compete with our students for university places, or for jobs. The government policy is to rid the children of their Indian-ness, to kill the Indian in the child, so to speak! Then to assimilate them on the bottom rung of the social ladder where they can do manual labour."

Father Thomas looked shocked.

And Mother Hall lost her airs and graces. "But we've got to keep 'em here 'til they're fifteen or sixteen? What the heck are we supposed to do with 'em?"

Mister Hall kicked his wife in the shins. "Let's not worry the governor about that, my dear."

"If you can teach them the basics of the three *R*'s," the governor continued, "Reading, 'Riting and 'Rithmetic, you will have achieved your mandate." He chuckled. "And, of course, Father Thomas, the fourth *R*: Religious studies!"

CHAPTER TWELVE

Turtle waited until all the boys in the dormitory were sleeping, then he slipped out of bed, and in his bare feet and nightgown crept out of the door and along the corridor to the staircase. The wooden steps creaked loudly. He stopped dead, heart pounding, but nobody came, and after a few seconds he tiptoed on.

It was coincidence that earlier in the day Turtle had been sent to Father Thomas's office at the same time as a girl from the other side of the school had been sent there. Turtle had done nothing wrong, at least he didn't think he had. He was merely delivering a written message. But he had walked slowly, head down, wondering if he would be able to complete his mission without getting punished. However, the girl who sat forlornly on the chair outside Father's Thomas's office, fingering a single strand of yellow yarn, knew for sure she would be punished. She knew exactly what she had done. It had been in sewing class. They had been making baby dolls, stuffing the cloth bodies with fluffy white blossoms of columbine then using strands of yarn for hair and red felt for lips. The girl had attached a pair of sky-blue glass buttons for eyes and held the finished doll at arm's length to admire her handiwork. The doll looked back at her with a quizzical expression. Emotion took the girl by surprise. Suddenly, her eyes were stinging and breath caught in her throat. She clutched the doll to her chest and sobbed as memories washed over her: a soft deerskin baby doll, a mother who hugged her.

"Put the doll in the donation box!"

The girl turned away.

"Look at me, girl! I said put it in the donation box. Now!"

The woman wrenched the doll away, leaving only a stand of yarn in the girl's clenched fingers.

"You ungrateful child!" she said, tossing it into the donation box. "These dolls are for deserving white children who don't have any toys to play with. Stop your snivelling, you bad girl. Go to the office!"

And so it was that when Turtle dawdled down the corridor with his message for Father Thomas, he was shocked to see the girl on the chair. This had never happened before. His apprehension vanished in a rush of excitement. "Do you know my sister, Willow?" he whispered urgently.

"You mean Anne? She is in my dormitory!"

"Tell me where."

The girl jutted her chin casually toward further down the corridor and murmured in a sing-song voice that could have been interpreted as a hum if anyone had overheard.

"Through that door, up two flights, third door."

Turtle whispered. "Tell her I'm coming ... tonight ... after lights out."

Turtle's clandestine route to Willow's dormitory took him down two flights of stairs, along the main floor corridor, past the grade one classroom and then past the offices. It was pitch black apart from the moonlight that shone through the barred windows, leaving a series of shadowy ladders emblazoned on the polished wood floor. When he saw the narrow shaft of lamplight that spilled from Mother Hall's door, fear stabbed his chest and made his heart pound. He hadn't anticipated that she would be there. Pinpoints of bright light flashed across his eyes and his knees buckled. He wanted to be back in his bed. But he couldn't turn back! Willow was waiting for him. The fainting spell passed, and on trembling legs he stole closer until he could peek through the gap in the door. Mother Hall sat close to the potbellied stove with a stack of envelopes on her lap. Turtle's heart was beating so violently that he feared Mother Hall would hear it.

"Little Deer," she mumbled, reading the name on an envelope. "Ain't got no Little Deer here." She tossed the envelope into the open lid of the stove and picked up another. "Can't even read the name on that one." The envelope went into the stove.

Turtle gasped. He had never received a letter from his parents in the two years he had been at the school, nor had any of the boys, as far as he knew. This was the reason! He wanted to scream at the top of his lungs that it was not fair, it was not right. He wanted to run to Willow and go home with her, but he didn't even know where home was! He had come to the school by train and wagon. It had taken days, through forests, across rivers. He would never find his way back. Besides, boys who ran away were nearly always brought back ... and beaten.

Mother Hall tossed another envelope toward the stove.

With that, he tiptoed across the wedge of lamp-light. A floorboard squeaked.

"Who's there?"

Turtle froze in the shadow, poised on his toes, scared to let out his breath in case she heard him. His knees began to shake. He knew he couldn't hold his position for long. It was all over! She would catch him! He would be whipped, and he would still not have seen his sister! A sound roared through his ears like the train that had brought him to school ... ker-chunk, ker-chunk, ker-chunk, ker-chunk. It took a second to realize that it was the pulsing of his own body.

Mother Hall turned her attention back to the stack of mail, throwing it piece by piece into the gaping mouth of the stove. Turtle exhaled as gently as he could and crept on, past Father Thomas's office to the big door that led to the girls' side of the building. He pushed the door but nothing happened. He pulled and pushed again with more strength, but still the door did not budge. His hands groped around the edges until, just above his head, he discovered a metal bolt. It flew back with a clunk that Turtle thought would wake the dead. He pushed open the door and left it standing ajar for his return trip. By the time he reached the bottom of the girls' staircase, he couldn't contain himself any longer. He didn't care if he was caught or what they would do to him. He bounded up the two flights of stairs and ran past the doors ... one ... two ...

There she was! Standing outside the door, waiting for him. He didn't need the dim moonlight to identify her, even though she was taller than he remembered. She flung her arms around him and held him tight, and he felt as though he was back in his mother's arms. He was warm inside and full, as though something deep inside his chest had grown bigger and could no longer be contained by bones and flesh and skin.

He barely heard the angry voices or saw the lamplight swinging down the corridor. They clung to each other as the cane crashed onto their backs. More staff arrived. It took the combined strength of five adults to wrench the children apart. Mister Hall almost lifted Turtle from the ground by his ear as he marched him away.

"You're going to have a beating like you've never had before."

All of the boys had to watch Turtle's punishment. His wrists were tied to the post in the courtyard. Mister Hall didn't use his cane. He used lots of rawhide straps joined together at the handle. Each piece of rawhide had a knot at the end. He hit Turtle over and over.

Often the older boys mocked the younger ones who were being punished, sneering at those who were forced to kneel in a corner, ridiculing those who had the striped haircut. But no one laughed when Turtle was being whipped, not even Henry. Red Wolf closed his eyes so he couldn't see, but his ears still heard the sound of the leather smacking into Turtle's skin, and the yelps that turned to moans and then to whimpers. He felt sick to his stomach.

Red Wolf didn't see Turtle for many days. The morning that he reappeared in the refectory,

Red Wolf was elated. But Turtle had changed. He was broken. The light in his eyes had gone.

CHAPTER THIRTEEN

The Grade One boys gathered around the farm manager in the hayfield. He was on edge. "There's enough grass in this field to feed the cows right through the winter," he said, "but we need a good, solid, dry spell to harvest it." He looked at the sky, trying to judge the weather.

Red Wolf felt the breeze on his face and was pretty sure that it wasn't going to rain for quite a while. He considered telling Mister Boss this, but thought better of it.

"Haymaking is tricky. Rain ruins hay! Even a passing shower makes it damp, and it'll grow mildew. Soon your sweet-smelling hay turns foul ... musty, full of grey dust ... makes the cows cough. But even worse than that, mouldy hay gets hot, really hot, so that it bursts into flames! I saw a whole barn go up once. It burned down in the blink of an eye, just because of mouldy hay. There wasn't even time to get inside and open the stall doors. The cows and horses burned, too."

The farm manager's face crumpled briefly, then he gnawed at the edge of a fingernail and continued with his haymaking lesson. "But if you wait too long for a dry spell, the grass goes to seed, and that's no good." He yanked at a grass stem and passed it to the boys. "See, it's perfect right now, just started to flower. We don't want to wait much longer." He looked at the children and singled one out. "And why don't we want to wait any longer?"

"I don't know, Mister Boss, sir," the worried boy said.

"Because once the grass flowers, the plant puts all its energy into making seed. The seeds fall off as soon as they are handled. And then what do we have?"

Nobody volunteered an answer.

"A barn full of tough old stalks. Understand?"

The boys nodded.

"Yes, haymaking's a tricky business."

After another two days of sunny weather the farm manager finally made a decision. He sent the seniors across the field in a row, each youth swinging a long-handled scythe. The grass fell in orderly lines, like columns of schoolboys who had their legs knocked out from underneath them.

The following day lessons were cancelled so that every boy in the school could help in the hayfield. Red Wolf advanced across the field, gathering day-old grass, flipping it over and laying it back down. He stooped until his back was so sore he couldn't straighten up, so he squatted and moved along on his haunches. Then he crawled on prayer-hardened knees with sweat stinging his eyes until the blazing sun disappeared over the horizon and the sky turned orange.

The following day, as soon as the dew burned off, they had to turn the hay again. Red Wolf ached all over, and his fingers were swollen and tender. When he squinted at them he saw fine thistle hairs embedded in his skin. He wondered how something so small could cause such discomfort.

It was hotter than the previous day, with not a cloud in the sky to offer a moment of shade.

"Haymaking and heat waves go hand in hand," the farm manager announced. "There's water in pails by the gate, but don't think you can shirk by going to get a drink any old time. I'll blow my whistle for a water break."

By the end of the second day Red Wolf flopped straight onto his bed without changing into his nightshirt. When Mother Hall came in for prayers, most of the boys were already sleeping.

The next day, the hay was dry and ready to be gathered, but the air was hot and humid, and there was a haze in the sky.

"There's a storm coming," the farm manager warned. "Move faster!"

The seniors ran into the field pulling hay wagons and the juniors loaded the hay. Red Wolf tossed hay as high as he could, but most of it never made it into the wagon; it rained down on his head and shoulders, getting in the neck of his coverall and making him itch.

By the time the seniors had pushed the loaded wagon up the earthen ramp of the bank barn, they were dripping with sweat, hair plastered to their heads. The juniors stayed in the oppressive heat of the loft, unloading and sneezing, while the seniors rushed downstairs, where thick stone walls held the night's coolness. They splashed themselves with water from the cattle trough until the farm manager complained they were wasting water. Then it was back to the field for another load.

Thunder was rolling in the distance as a Belgian mare the colour of rich honey trotted briskly across the hay field, a large empty wagon clanking behind her.

"I thought you could use some help," the driver called out to the boys as he slowed the horse to a walk and guided her carefully through the rows of hay. "Load her up fast, rain's on the way."

The boys ran across the field like ants to a carcass, grabbing armloads of hay and flinging them up onto the moving wagon, their fatigue vanishing with the excitement. The horse sensed their eagerness and shook her head, jangling her harness buckles.

"Hi there, neighbour," the farm manager called out. "How did you know we needed help?"

"From my place I saw these kids crawling all over the field. And I heard the thunder so I put two and two together. I've told you before, my friend, and I'll tell you again. This school needs a good workhorse."

The farm manager laughed. "Why do we need a horse when we have all these boys?"

"You could use one today," the neighbour commented, disturbed as always by the subdued Indian children who worked as hard as grown men.

The horse pulled the final wagonload under cover just as fat raindrops started to spatter. The two men sheltered in the barn as thunder crashed and lightning forked angrily across the dark sky, but, unmindful of the danger, the boys stood in the pouring rain, letting the deluge cool them. One decided to strip his coveralls, another his boots, another his under-drawers. Before long the entire student body was leaping around stark naked, stomping in puddles and dancing in the sheets of water falling from the roof.

As the rain petered out, the farm manager poked his head out to look at the sky. He was appalled.

"What are you doing?" he yelled. "Cavorting like savages?"

The old man laughed. "No, they're cavorting like children!"

The farm manager ignored him. "Have you all gone mad? Get your clothes back on before Father Thomas sees you."

"They're just being boys," the old man said to the wind.

A few days after the hay was safely in the barn, impatient boys clustered around the barred windows that overlooked the driveway. They watched other children pile into the neighbour's wagon that would take them to the train station and the long journey back to their reserves. And they stared into the distance, hoping that the next person to come into view would be their mother or father, big brother, or uncle. As the day progressed, the number of children at the windows decreased and, for those who remained, excitement turned first to apprehension and then to fear that nobody would come for them.

Mother Hall strode past the small group of remaining boys. "Are you still waiting?" she asked. "Perhaps your parents don't want you no more. Heaven knows you're a whole lot of trouble. I wouldn't want you if I didn't get paid for the job."

It was late afternoon when Mister Hall strutted along the corridor, his cane lightly tapping the side of his leg with each footfall. He whacked Red Wolf on the side of the head.

"So your no-good father hasn't shown up, eh?"

Red Wolf was silent, but then realized that an answer was expected. "No, Mister Hall."

"Do you suppose he's lying drunk in a ditch?"

"Yes, Mister Hall. No, Mister Hall. I don't know, Mister Hall."

"He probably spent all his ration money on drink and can't even walk straight."

Mister Hall guffawed, thwacking the heads of the other two boys who waited with Red Wolf, then strode off down the corridor.

The shadows were lengthening when Father Thomas stopped to talk to Red Wolf and the one remaining boy. The priest tutted at the wayward behaviour of Indian parents.

"Such degenerate conduct! Imagine neglecting your own children in such a manner. This is the very reason we take you from your families: to spare you this pain of rejection; to feed you, clothe you and give you the opportunity to better yourselves."

Tears welled in Red Wolf's eyes.

"It hurts me to see you so disappointed. It's George, isn't it?"

"Yes, Father."

"Believe me, George, you are better off without them. I know you feel hurt, but suffering is part of growing up. Suffering will mold you into a better person. Wait and see." Father Thomas rocked back on his heels and looked upward. "We learn from our pain, George. We cannot taste joy until we have drunk from the cup of sorrow."

The priest was pleased with this analogy. Then he had another thought, and he beamed. "Just think, George, if you had not shivered through the cold, dark days of winter, you would not truly appreciate the warmth and light of summer."

He patted the boy's head and continued down the corridor, mentally composing his next sermon, which, he realized sadly, would not be until September.

Just before dark, the nurse came down the corridor and saw one lonely figure, his face pressed close to the pane of glass. "Oh, you poor dear," she said. "Are you still waiting for your family?"

"They don't want me," Red Wolf replied, his downcast face hiding the tears that stung his eyes.

The nurse knelt and looked into the boy's tear-stained face. "Oh, surely not!"

"They've forgotten me."

"Heavens, that's not true. How could anyone forget a boy like you?" She took a clean handkerchief from her apron pocket and wiped Red Wolf's tears.

"So why haven't they come for me?"

"Sometimes they can't get permission to leave the reserve," she explained sadly, "so they can't come for you, even if they really, really want to."

"What happens to me if no one comes?" the boy asked very quietly, as if scared to voice his concern.

"The big boys go into town. They work for white families in exchange for their keep. But the younger ones, like you, stay on here. They have to work for —" looking over both shoulders she whispered "— evil Mother Hall." She pounced on Red Wolf in a spree of tickling and the boy giggled.

Red Wolf looked down the driveway one more time and saw his father shrouded in the dusk. "He's here! He's here!" the boy shrieked, bolting for the staircase and running outside. He threw himself into his father's open arms, nearly knocking over HeWhoWhistles. And even though he was happier than he had been for ten long months, he wept. The nurse watched from the window and cried, too.

Red Wolf wanted to walk all night, to get as far away from the school as he could, but HeWhoWhistles had already walked all day and needed to sleep. They stopped where a brook ran through a field. Red Wolf didn't want to sleep in case he woke up and found himself back at school, but within minutes of nestling into his father's chest, feeling his warm skin and listening to his heartbeat, he was sleeping dreamlessly.

He awoke at dawn to the melody of a songbird.

"*Aaniish ezhi baked?*" HeWhoWhistles asked.

Red Wolf looked blankly at his father.

"*Nwii-mwaa giigoonh.*"

The boy still did not respond.

"Why do you not understand me?" HeWho-Whistles asked. "What have they done to you?"

Red Wolf did not recall the words to tell his father that it didn't matter if they couldn't understand each other, it was enough just to be together.

HeWhoWhistles waded into the brook with a sharpened stick. "*Giigoohn,*" he said, "*Wiisnin giigoohn.*"

"Yes!" Red Wolf said excitedly. "*Wiisnin gii-goohn.*"

HeWhoWhistles smiled.

The brook trout was the most satisfying meal that Red Wolf had eaten in ten months. When they reached the edge of the forest, his spirits lifted even more. The trees surrounded him in soft green light. He felt safe. Not even the mosquitoes that buzzed in his ears and bit at his skin could spoil his mood. Summer stretched ahead of him. It would last forever.

A wet nose slid under his hand. He turned to run, but then he saw Crooked Ear. The wolf was no longer a gangling pup. He stood as tall as the boy's shoulder, but his left ear was still crooked. The expression in his eyes was still the same, and Red Wolf recognized him instantly.

Crooked Ear trembled, wanting to roll on the ground with the child as he would with another wolf, but something warned him that the Upright pup needed to be treated gently. So he raced in circles until he was calm enough to sit on his haunches and allow the child to throw his arms around him. He licked behind the boy's ear, Red Wolf's giggles making the animal's tail swish back and forth.

Then they chased each other along the trail. On the steep hills the boy held on to Crooked Ear's ruff and allowed the wolf to pull him up the incline. Then they both raced down the other side, the wolf taking the lead and the boy, with arms held wide, pretending to fly like a bird.

But as night fell and HeWhoWhistles made camp, the wolf faded into the night and Red Wolf snuggled into the warmth of his father.

CHAPTER FOURTEEN

Red Wolf's heart had ached for ten months to return to his family. Now that he was home he was disappointed. Everything was strange. It was as if they had sent him back to the wrong home, the wrong family.

In his memory, home was a fur-lined, birch-bark *wiigwam*. The reality was a shack made of pine boards topped with a rusting metal roof. It reminded him of the potting shed at school where dead children, it was said, waited for spring when they would be planted in the ground. Red Wolf's baby sister had made a stunning transformation from a helpless infant to a boisterous, inquisitive little girl. She could walk and even talk, although he could not understand her words — but at first he couldn't understand anyone's words, not even his mother's. And when he spoke in English, they looked at him with blank stares.

He still didn't understand why he had been sent away to school. His father had said they had no choice, that it was the white man's law. But Red Wolf believed that his father could defy Father Thomas, and the Halls, and the Indian agent, and all the laws that the white man had set in place, if he wanted to.

Father Thomas had given the children a summer assignment, to turn their parents away from the sinful, savage ways that led to Hell, and guide them instead on the path to Jesus. Red Wolf had not completely understood the lesson, and Father Thomas's words did not easily translate into *Anishnaabemowin*, which was beginning to return to him. However, the boy had learned quite thoroughly that he was a filthy Indian and a savage. The knowledge had left him feeling sullied and ashamed. If he told his parents that they too were filthy Indians and savages, they would be dishonoured and ashamed also.

An unnatural silence settled over the family. When they spoke to him, he answered in monosyllables, or not at all. But Red Wolf was comfortable with silence. He had learned over the past year that silence usually meant safety. For his parents, however, the silence in the small cabin was deafening.

StarWoman didn't know what was wrong with her son and didn't know how to fix it. She ached to hold him in her arms as she had when he was a baby, but he was cool in response to her warmth. He was getting bigger, she mused, too big to be treated like a toddler. His baby skin had started to change even before he had gone away to school.

It bore the marks of growing up, of moving out into the world beyond her constant protection. But there were other marks on his skin now that she thought must have come from rough play with the boys at school. When she pointed and asked about them, he pushed her hand away and remained silent. StarWoman struggled to accept that her firstborn was growing up. It saddened her that she was being left behind. She gave her daughter the hugs she longed to give her son.

HeWhoWhistles, aware that his son had entered a new world, took sanctuary in the outdoors. Sometimes Red Wolf joined his father in the bush, and wherever the boy went, Crooked Ear followed, bounding in and out of the bushes or ambling along with the child's hand resting on his back. HeWhoWhistles felt that the wolf understood his son better than he did, and when the creature melted back into the forest, leaving him alone with Red Wolf, he was uncomfortable. They walked close, but there was distance between them.

"What did you learn at the white man's school?" HeWhoWhistles blurted out one day, not really expecting an answer.

Red Wolf was refamiliarizing himself with *Anishnaabemowin*, but the answers to his father's question formed in his head in English, not in his mother tongue.

I learned to never talk in Anishnaabemowin.

I learned to be quiet and not draw attention to myself.

I learned to never let my pain, or my fear, or my anger show on my face.

I learned that I am a savage.

That The People are heathens and pagans.

That we are all dirty Indians.

I learned that if they educate us and cut our hair and give us white boys' clothes, and if we say we love Jesus ... then we will be saved. We will no longer be dirty Indians. But I don't know what we shall be. I don't think we shall ever be white boys.

I learned to hide inside myself and pretend I wasn't there.

I learned to bury my head in the pillow and shut my eyes and pretend I couldn't see, or hear, or feel the things that were happening in the night.

He shuddered then answered his father in the language of The People, which rolled slowly from his tongue.

"I learned about Jesus."

"Who is Jesus?"

"A good white man."

HeWhoWhistles looked dubious.

"He smiles ... almost," Red Wolf added.

"Does he teach you the scratchy lines?"

"No!" the boy replied. "Jesus is dead. His head is on the wall at school!"

HeWhoWhistles was confused. "His head?"

"Yes, father. Like a picture drawn in the sand. He is son of their chief, son of Father Thomas, I think." A frown spread over the boy's brow. "But he must have been bad, because they nailed him to a tree, like this." Red Wolf spread his hands and dropped his head on his chest.

HeWhoWhistles was skeptical, wondering if his son had learned the white man's lesson correctly. But he remembered the sacred story of *Nanabozho* and the Great Spirit Wolf. He reflected that *Nanabozho* and *Ma'een'gun* had disobeyed Creator and as a result there were consequences for eternity; wolf and man had been set on separate paths, their close bond broken. Maybe Creator had punished Jesus in the same way.

While HeWhoWhistles pondered this, Red Wolf was mentally translating his next thoughts into the language of The People.

"Jesus looks like you, father. He has long hair and doe eyes."

Understanding lit HeWhoWhistles' face. "That is why they killed him! They do not like The True People, or ones that look like us."

Red Wolf nodded his agreement. "Father Thomas says, 'Believe Jesus, or go to Hell.'"

HeWhoWhistles frowned. "Where is Hell? Is it a reserve?"

"Hell is a bad *wiigwam* under the earth. The fire in Hell-*wiigwam* is hot. It smells bad. The people in

Hell-*wiigwam* cry forever. *ForEverAndEverAmen,*" he added in English.

"Can they not throw open the door flap?" HeWhoWhistles asked.

"No, they never get out! It's their place in the spirit world forever."

HeWhoWhistles pondered his son's words for a long time, his breath moving in rhythm with his soft footfalls. "My son, the white man makes this life very hard for us. I am not yet dead, but already I am in Hell! They can do no more to me."

Father and son walked on in silence, heads down, eyes on their moving feet. HeWhoWhistles reached down and plucked a stem of horsetail. Absently he pulled it in two, feeling the spray of water that sprang from the break. He handed one half to Red Wolf and used the other to thoughtfully scrape his teeth. Red Wolf did the same.

"Did you learn the scratchy lines?" HeWho-Whistles asked after a while.

"Yes."

"Then, son, you will make sure we are not lied to again."

August came to a close. HeWhoWhistles had been given a ten-day pass and was ready to walk his son back to school. Red Wolf said goodbye to his mother with little emotion. He saw the grief on her face, but he was angry they were sending him back, and he didn't want to give her the satisfaction of a tearful goodbye.

When they reached the place where the forest met the meadow, Crooked Ear would go no further. Red Wolf understood that this was the moment to say goodbye. He grasped the wolf around the neck and buried his head in the warm, thick coat, breathing in the lupine odour. Tears came unexpectedly and furiously. He let them seep into the wolf's fur.

CHAPTER FIFTEEN

Red Wolf settled back into the routine of being George.

Henry moved up to Grade Two along with George, and the older boy never missed an opportunity to torment the younger. Henry would give George a swift kick on his backside when the teacher wasn't looking; he would steal George's slate or his chalk and try in all manner of ways to get him into trouble with the teacher. He did all this while telling George he was a stupid Indian.

George longed to tell Henry that *he* was the stupid Indian because *he* still had to go to the Grade One classroom during lunch break for remedial reading lessons with Master Evans. But George kept quiet because he was intimidated, not just by Henry's size but by his spitefulness.

During his education thus far, George had learned as much about chickens as he had about reading, writing, and arithmetic, so it was plain to him that the pecking order in the chicken coop was no different from the pecking order in the school. The top chicken asserted its dominance by pecking at another chicken, who rarely fought back. Instead it turned on the next one down the line. At the very bottom of the order the lowliest bird became balder and balder as more and more feathers were plucked out. Once blood was drawn the hens ganged up, drilling at the blood spots in a manner that reminded George of a woodpecker hammering at a tree. They attacked the lowly hen until it lay featherless and bloody and dead.

Before coming to school George would have empathized with the victimized bird and would have tried to stop the carnage, but his tender heart had hardened, and his childish desire to help the helpless and rectify injustice had been replaced with a cold neutrality. It was as if his heart and mind were detached from what his eyes saw. He accepted the pecking order in the school just as he accepted it in the chicken coop. He watched strong boys bully weaker ones, who in turn bullied those who were weaker still. In George's world, Henry was at the top of the pecking order. And since George had no intention of ending up at the bottom he did his fair share of bullying, too.

The Grade Two teacher was called Sir. When children couldn't answer Sir's questions, he made them kneel in a pan of grit. Henry knelt there more than anyone else. His knees were almost always pockmarked. This was one of the few things that gave George any gratification.

George hated Henry! It was as simple as that.

Until he had started school, he hadn't hated anyone or anything. He had sometimes been impatient and occasionally angry, but these were short-lived moods, not the all-encompassing hatred that festered in him now. He hated school. He hated the routines. He hated the staff. But more than all these things he hated Henry.

George wished with all his heart that Henry would die.

Sickness arrived with the winter, rampaging through the school like wildfire. Henry was one of the first to be taken to the infirmary. George was elated! For once in his life, something he wished for might come true: Henry was sick. All he had to do now was die! But Henry recovered quickly and came back to class. That same day, Turtle's face was flushed with fever and Mother Hall sent him straight to the infirmary. George was distraught. He was convinced that the God of the School was punishing him for wishing such wickedness on Henry. He prayed to Godthefather-Godtheson-and-Godtheholyspirit, asking forgiveness for being such a stupid savage and such an ungrateful sinner, and begging that Turtle would get better.

Healthy children were banned from going anywhere close to the infirmary, but George broke the rule and sneaked into the corridor in the hope of seeing Turtle. He was shocked when he saw the large number of beds that spilled out of the infirmary and were lined up in the corridor. More children were sick than he had realized. He didn't see Turtle.

"You can't be here!" the nurse exclaimed. "You'll catch the sickness."

"Is Turtle here ... 298?" George asked, backing away.

The nurse looked very sad. "You have to leave right now, George."

"Is he here?" George insisted.

"No. He's gone."

"Where's he gone?" George asked.

The nurse had tears in her eyes. "He's not in pain anymore, George. He's home."

George was relieved.

The young nurse barely slept. She worked around the clock. The job at Bruce County Indian Residential School was her first job since training and she so wanted to nurse the children back to health, but there were too many children and she was overwhelmed. She longed to get away, to go home to her mother and father. In desperation she went down on her knees and with tears brimming from her closed eyes she prayed, "God, find me a way out."

She had never heard the voice of God, and she didn't expect a verbal answer, but in her heart she suddenly knew that she had to stay with the children, to treat their ailments as best she could, but more importantly to comfort them and hold their hands and be with them when their sad souls left their bodies. She promised herself that no child would die alone, unnoticed. She prayed that God would help her.

The nurse was too busy with the living and the dying to know that the dead were taken, unceremoniously, to the potting shed in a wheelbarrow. Mother Hall wrote the tags that Mister Hall then wired onto the big toes of the cold corpses. If, during its short life, a child had imprinted itself onto the mind of a staff member, a Christian name was written on the toe-tag, but those who had not been particularly memorable went to "heaven" with the same identity they had lived by: a number.

Initially the bodies were placed in rough-sawn pine boxes, stacked from the ground up to economize on space. Rakes, hoes, shovels, and forks once spread at random throughout the shed were leaned up against the stacked boxes with a semblance of order. But when the carpenter could no longer keep pace with the demand for coffins, the bodies, wrapped in sheets, were placed directly on the slatted tables. They remained there, guarded by rat traps, until the ground thawed in the spring.

For a while George believed that Turtle had gone home to his parents, but one day in religious knowledge class, Father Thomas referred to Heaven as "Our Eternal Home."

There was a jolt inside George's chest. And he knew the truth.

The next morning when Mother Hall came to the dormitory, Red Wolf raised his hand and waited until she permitted him to speak.

"Please, Mother, I ask for haircut."

Everyone looked at him as if he had gone mad.

Mother Hall smiled with delight. "Of course, 366. Tomorrow is haircut day for this dormitory, so you won't have to wait much longer."

The following day, as his hair fell to the ground, Red Wolf closed his eyes tight to prevent the spill of tears and, in the way of The People, he said goodbye to his friend.

Spring came. The afternoon sun beat down on the shiny metal roof of the potting shed, releasing the faintest scent of death through the cracks in the timbers. But the nights were still cool and an early morning fog settled over the grounds of Bruce County School. It dampened the coveralls of the gaunt youths who wielded long-handled shovels. The Indian agent's dog joined them as they dug, scrabbling vigorously with his front paws, sending dirt flying through his hind legs. A safe distance away, three ravens attempted to alight on the same wooden cross. They jockeyed for dominance, flapping and squawking until the cross gave way and collapsed onto the grass, sending the birds back into the air.

They flew in a circle of reconnaissance, landing this time on a rectangular box that lay untended on the grass. United in a common task, they pecked at the wood, pulling fibres away with their strong beaks and claws. The smell, barely discernible to human senses, drove them into a frenzy of activity. But their efforts were thwarted. Father Thomas appeared at the back door of the school and lumbered toward the birds, waving his arms and shouting. The dog joined the chase, forcing the ravens to disappear into the mist. They retreated to the safety of the roof, where they preened and waited. But this was not their lucky day, and before the sun had burned away the mist, the corpses had been buried deep in the ground.

Father Thomas added the final touches. He smoothed the fresh mounds of soil with the back of the shovel and pushed newly cut pine crosses into the soft dirt. He frowned, annoyed that the sap from the fresh wood was sticking to his hands. He took a handkerchief from his pocket and tried to rub off the resin, but it only smeared. Sighing, he crossed himself and beseeched God to save the souls of the little savages. Then he went about his day.

CHAPTER SIXTEEN

The previous September, when Red Wolf returned to school to start Grade Two, Crooked Ear had lingered again at the edge of the forest. After several days he seemed to understand that the boy was not coming back, so he turned his nose south and let instinct take him back to Clear Lake. Seraph was not pleased to see his nephew, driving him away from the pack as before and allowing him to live only on the fringe until Crooked Ear had once again displayed complete subservience.

The cold months passed and finally the frozen lake began to thaw, and the wolves basked again in the sun on the granite outcrop high on the ridge. Seraph's second litter was born, and it was then that Crooked Ear's legs became restless and he felt the urge to move on. When the trilliums faded on the forest floor and new leaves unfurled on the maples, he trotted away from Clear Lake, drawn once more to the place where instinct told him the boy would reappear. And there he waited.

When the scent of the little Upright drifted to his twitching nostrils, Crooked Ear yipped and quivered with excitement.

Red Wolf, too, was overjoyed to see his friend again. When he nestled his face into the wolf's fur, the turmoil inside of him became still. But the boy's reunion with his parents did not have the same calming effect. In their presence he felt stirred up inside and he behaved in ways that he didn't understand. It was as if he was a pot of stew boiling over the fire. Great globs splattered over the edge, burning whatever they landed on.

His parents still called him *Mishqua Ma'een'gun*. It was *Mishqua Ma'een'gun* this, and *Mishqua Ma'een'gun* that, until finally he blurted out, "Don't call me that. I'm George. Are you stupid? Why can't you remember? Say it, say George."

HeWhoWhistles and StarWoman were speechless, their mouths agape, dismayed at the anger that spewed from their son's mouth along with the foreign words.

He spelled out the name. "G-E-O-R-G-E."

There was no response.

George continued his tirade, unable to stop. "Mister Hall is right," he yelled, "You are all ignorant savages. There's no point in trying to teach you anything because you'll always be stupid."

The boy felt as though he was canoeing through white water … alone … without a paddle.

He wanted to get out of the wild river, but he couldn't. It was running too fast, and he was being carried helplessly along.

George looked into his mother's face and knew he had gone too far. Shame flooded him. It was even worse than the shame he felt every day at school. He ran from the cabin into the bush, unable to look at them another moment, wanting only to escape from the feelings that roiled inside him.

Part of him wished that summer would last forever, but there was another part of him that wished it would be over right away. But as with everything else in his life, he had no control, and in due course hot days gave way to colder nights. And fingers of foreboding clutched his gut.

HeWhoWhistles walked his son back to school. It was a sad procession of man, child, and wolf. Each walked silently, heavily, as though he had a great weight on his shoulders.

Grade Three was no easier than Grade Two, or Grade One. Henry was still in George's class, but there was a new boy, too. He was light-skinned and had sandy brown hair and eyes flecked with green. He was almost as pale as the teacher, but George knew the boy couldn't be white because the teacher whacked his fair head even more than he whacked his own. The new boy was *half-breed*. George and the others were *full-breed*, and they taunted the *half-breed* because he was different and because they all knew that a half is less than a whole.

In late autumn the Grade Three boys were turning over Mother Hall's flowerbeds at the front of the school. The neighbouring farmer guided his mare through the gate, and as soon as the farm cart rolled to a stop, George climbed into the back and started shovelling manure into waiting barrows.

The old man watched the boys working and his heart was troubled. He studied the one with sombre eyes who stood in the wagon, briskly shovelling manure, and he wondered how the boy had got the bruise on his cheek, and what secrets were hidden behind his expressionless face.

A grey jay flew overhead, swooping between the bars of an opening in the wall and hitting the glass with a thud.

Everyone turned to watch as it fluttered to the ground and lay still.

"Poor thing," Mother Hall said, peering closely at the bird, "it probably broke its neck."

The boys gathered around and stared.

George was suddenly attentive to every detail. The gate was open, and Mother Hall was distracted. He looked at the old man who sat in the driver's seat of the cart, the reins loose in his hands. Much to George's surprise the man looked right back at him, then stood and lifted the seat, nodding toward a hiding place beneath. George's heart raced. *Does he want to help me, or is it a trap?*

The jay suddenly revived, flopping around in the dirt for a few seconds, then flying in dazed circles around Mother Hall's head. She ducked, shielding her head with her hands and screeching. The jay screeched too and the boys burst into gales of laughter.

"Pssst," the old man hissed.

George did not hesitate. He dived under the seat and curled into a ball. The lid dropped and the old man clucked. "Git along."

The cart jolted forward. Above the sound of his pounding heart, George heard the mare's hooves clomping on the gravel, the jangle of the harness, and the creak of the wheels.

For a while the old man whistled, then mumbled words the boy could not hear.

"What made you go and do that, you old fool? If Hall finds out, you can say goodbye to the work the school gives you, and the extra money that goes along with it. You're a stupid old coot!" He laughed aloud. "But it sure feels good! Gets the old heart beating!"

He raised his voice. "How are you doing down there, child? I can't take you much further. I've got to hook up the other cart and get back. If I keep them busy they won't miss you 'til later. By that time you'll have a good head start."

The horse stopped in front of the barn and the old man climbed down, lifting the seat to help George out.

"Come with me, I'll get you some supplies."

In the farmhouse the old man wrapped a hunk of cheese in a square muslin cloth and stuffed it into a leather bag along with half a loaf of bread and a tin of matches.

"Do you know how to work these?" he asked.

George shook his head.

The old man opened the box and struck one of the small sticks against the rough strip on the edge of the box. George jumped back when the stick burst into flames.

"Keep 'em dry and they'll work fine." He closed the little tin and put it in the bag, passing the strap over the boy's head and straightening it over his shoulder. "Do you know your way home?" he asked.

The boy nodded.

"Good. But remember, they'll send someone after you, probably the Indian agent and his dog. Go through water to throw the hound off your scent, and when you get home lay low, or they'll fetch you right back here in no time."

The old man was beginning to regret his rash decision. The boy would never make it! He'd be caught and brought back, and no doubt punished. And if the boy implicated him in the escape ...

"If they catch you, don't say I helped you. Say you ran through the open gate."

The thought of being caught had not entered into George's head when he dived under the seat of the old man's wagon. But now, suddenly, he was terrified. *They'll catch me. I'll get whipped, like Turtle was.* The strength drained from his legs as if the bones had softened.

A jumble of thoughts crowded into his head. *Even if I get home, Father will send me back to school! Unless we leave the reserve and go back to Clear Lake, or some place where the white man doesn't live.* Another idea came to him. *I'll live with Crooked Ear.* But deep down he knew it wouldn't have worked. For one thing, he didn't know where the wolf was or how to find him. And then he berated himself. *You are so stupid!*

The prospect of being whipped like Turtle weighed heavily on his heart, and his courage failed him. *If I go back to school right now maybe I won't be punished too badly, maybe not at all. They may not even know that I am gone.*

He was about to tell the man that he had changed his mind and ask if he could go back to the school the same way as he had come, hidden under the seat, but the old man was handing him a rabbit-skin jacket. "Try this on."

The jacket came down below the boy's knees, like a coat. It was warm, but more than that, it was comforting, like sitting next to a friend. It made him feel better.

Cuffing the sleeves to make them shorter, the old man stood back to look at the effect. "The nights are getting cold and the snow will soon be here. You need to get home fast or you'll freeze." He led George outside. Hundreds of small black birds swarmed overhead. Moving individually and yet as a single unit, they veered to one side of the sky and then back to the other, the edges of the formation becoming ragged for no more than a second.

"The birds know that winter's almost here, so go quickly," the old man said, taking a hunting knife from his belt and holding it out. "And take this."

He stiffly bent over and gently lifted the boy's downturned face to meet his own. "God go with you, son."

George felt a warm glow in his chest. It was a sensation that he hadn't experienced for a long time.

CHAPTER SEVENTEEN

Top Boy Frank was the only one to see George disappear under the seat of the cart. He didn't tell. Other boys gradually became aware of George's absence, and by bedtime everyone in the junior dormitory knew. They all ran the risk of punishment for aiding and abetting, but despite this they agreed to bundle clothes into the empty bed and cover them with the blanket. It fooled Mother Hall, who had become increasingly lax with bedtime prayers. She turned out the lights without suspecting a thing.

It wasn't until the following morning when the boys knelt at their bedsides that the absence of 366 was apparent. All the boys in the Grade Three work crew and those in the junior dormitory were threatened, caned, and threatened some more, but none of them was able to tell when, where, or how George had made his escape, because none of them knew what had happened.

By midday the Indian agent arrived, the mid-section of his horse barely visible under the supplies. He was whistling a tune, delighted at the prospect of tracking a child. He enjoyed the challenge of pursuit.

Mother Hall gave him George's crumpled night-shirt. He offered it to the dog. "Take a good sniff. That's who we're after."

The dog wagged his tail enthusiastically. The agent tried to pack the nightshirt into his already overstuffed saddlebags, but then tore off a strip and pushed it deep into the pocket of his coat.

He yanked the saddle's cinch a few inches tighter and refastened it, the horse announcing his displeasure by raising a hind hoof and flattening his ears. Then the agent loosened his own belt buckle, letting it out to the final hole so that his trousers slung comfortably underneath his belly.

"He's got an overnight head start," Mother Hall warned.

The Indian agent put his foot in the stirrup and started to haul himself into the saddle. "You know I always bring 'em back. So which one am I after?"

"Three-six-six."

"Horse Thief!" he exclaimed, dropping his weight heavily and causing the horse to grunt. A large grin spread across the agent's face. "Mrs. Hall, I'm going to really enjoy catching this one. Nobody gets away from me, and especially not Horse Thief."

Mother Hall waved. "Good luck."

"Aw, luck has nothing to do with it," he replied, passing through the gate and pushing the horse into a gentle canter. "It's skill, my dear, pure skill."

At first the hound was unable to pick up the scent, but the agent guessed the boy would head home, so he took the trail toward the reserve. He was not blind to the spectacular scenery around him. The fall colours were past their peak, but a few fragile leaves still clung to the branches, and occasional splashes of orange and scarlet fluttered back and forth like Monarch butterflies. He looked up at the clear blue sky and reflected on the beauty of this vast land he now called home. How clean everything was compared with the squalor of London. He rarely thought of his previous life, but now he cast his mind back to the one room his whole family had lived in, so close to the Thames that at low tide the stink of slimy mud pervaded even the smell of frying sausages.

He wondered what his brothers were doing, what he himself would be doing had he not had the guile to cheat another young man out of his boat passage to the new land. He congratulated himself on his accomplishment. Never again would he doff his hat at landed gentry. Having to learn the peculiar Algonquian language in order to communicate with the savages was a small price to pay.

With the sun on his shoulders, the rustle of leaves underfoot, and the smell of horse sweat rising to his nostrils, an uncharacteristic peace settled on his soul. He breathed deeply and sighed. Life was good.

The hound, having found no scent of the quarry, turned to chasing squirrels. But as soon as he caught the boy's scent, he forgot all about the squirrels and ran with his nose to the ground.

Horse and rider followed, swinging into an easy canter that ate up the miles. When they reached the place where the boy had left the trail to make a fire and sleep for the night, the agent dismounted and stretched while the dog sniffed at the depression in the vegetation. The agent didn't see the second depression a little deeper into the tangled bush, but the dog had found it at once, enticed by the strong odour that was almost canine, yet wild. It made him tremble. He clamped his tail firmly between his legs.

"Come on, dog. The boy's long gone."

The hound was soon following the boy's scent again, all fear forgotten. He moved fast, racing ahead of horse and rider, who were struggling to keep up. Suddenly he slithered to a halt and backed up. The same wild smell was all around him. It was overpowering. His hackles rose and he bolted back down the trail with a yelp.

The horse stopped dead, shied sideways, and wheeled to the left.

"What the —"

The Indian agent thudded painfully to the ground and the panicked horse galloped toward home. Cursing, the man picked up his hat and slammed it furiously against his leg. Unless he could catch his horse it was going to be a very long walk home.

It was then that he saw the wolf, bigger and redder than any wolf he had ever seen. The animal was half concealed in the bush not ten yards away, staring intently with amber eyes, one ear erect, the other bent in half. In the animal's cautious but inquisitive gaze the man discerned violence and savagery.

He reached for his gun, but it wasn't there — it was on the horse! He wanted to run, but his knees were buckling and he knew the great creature would be upon him in a single bound. He'd heard that wolves couldn't climb trees, so he looked around for one with low branches, but fear of fangs tearing at his nether regions kept him on the ground. He was totally powerless and he knew it. He stood on shaking legs, contemplating his death and the pain that might be involved.

He urinated in his trousers.

As quickly as it had appeared, the wolf was gone.

The sun was low in the sky when the farm carts bumped down the rutted street and pulled into the town square. The Indian agent was waiting for them, rubbing the bruise on his rear end. It hadn't taken him long to find his horse, nibbling grass at the side of the trail. Worried that the wolf might reappear, he had mounted up immediately and ridden as fast as his sore backside allowed to the nearest town, plotting revenge on the creature that dared to terrorize and humiliate him.

"I'm afraid to tell you —" he started, raising his voice and holding up his hands until the small crowd paid attention "— that one of them poor little Injun run-a-ways from the Bruce County School just got eaten by a wolf."

The women's hands flew to their mouths.

"I tried to save the boy. I did the best I could. But out of nowhere a whole pack of wolves showed up and ripped that poor boy limb from limb!"

He dug in his pocket for the ragged strip of nightgown that he had stained with earth and squashed tomato. He held it aloft. "In no time there was nothing left but this!"

The crowd was aghast. The Indian agent had them right where he wanted them.

"Now they've had a taste of Injun-boy blood, they'll be back for more. They'll come for *our* babies and *our* children."

Suddenly everyone was talking at once, their voices angry and insistent.

"I shot two wolves last month," a man shouted.

"The bounty's gonna come in real handy."

"Trouble is," the agent continued, "the varmints keep breeding faster than we can get rid of 'em. So what I've got here —" he paused, holding a tin box above his head and waiting for the curiosity of the crowd to pique "— is poison bait."

"Won't that kill other animals, too?"

"Nothing we can't live without," the Indian agent replied. "Fox, raccoon, bear."

"I just lost six hens to a fox!" shouted a farmer. "The darned critter ate only one of 'em. Left the other five dead on the henhouse floor! Where am I gonna get more laying hens at this time of year?"

"I got extras. Reckon I could sell you a few —"

The agent interrupted before the meeting degenerated into a buy-and-sell session. "Over in South Fork they used this stuff, and there ain't a single wolf left. Their children are safe. Yes, their children —" he paused for dramatic effect "— are safe."

"The only good wolf is a dead wolf!" a farmer yelled, and the crowd roared its approval.

CHAPTER EIGHTEEN

When George saw the still water of Boulder Lake glistening in the late afternoon sun, relief poured over him. His feet and legs ached from two days of walking and running, but he was more than halfway home.

Crooked Ear had been travelling with the boy for several hours and eagerly loped forward to quench his thirst, his front feet submerged, his long pink tongue lapping noisily. The boy threw himself face down on the warm granite and scooped water into his mouth, then unpacked his bag and looked at the small piece of bread and cheese that remained. He divided it, rewrapped half, and nibbled on the remainder.

The wolf sat on his haunches watching, head cocked, one ear pricked, strings of drool dangling from the corners of his mouth.

The boy unwrapped the cheese again and gave the wolf a sliver. "This is all I have," he said, his voice tinged with regret. "Go and catch something to eat."

The October sun, which had lazily made its way across the sky, suddenly fell into the shining lake. The boy called out to Crooked Ear, but the wolf had wandered away in search of food, and he was alone. Hoping a fire would protect and comfort him, he quickly gathered kindling in the gloom. Squatting low to the ground, he struck a match and fed the tiny blaze with twigs, listening to the pops and hisses.

One of the sticks was green and flexible and, as he held it in his hands, he envisioned it as a dream catcher. He remembered the one that had hung over his head in the *wiigwam* so he would have only good dreams. Bad dreams had plagued him at school, and now that he was alone in the wilderness he feared his dreams would be even worse. He hunched close to the firelight and twisted the stick into a circle. Without sinew, he used grass and plant stems to create the mesh that would trap the bad dreams. He looked critically at the finished object. It was flimsy, an oval, not a circle, and the hole that allowed the good dreams to pass through was off-centre. Hoping it would be better than nothing, he hung it from a branch not far from the dying embers and curled up underneath. But he couldn't sleep. The noises of the night became sinister in his solitude: the rustling of a roosting bird; a twig spiralling to the ground; a bat flitting through the branches.

Then, close by, he heard an animal snuffling in the undergrowth. His body went rigid with fear and he held his breath. Sure that it was the agent's dog, he willed himself to remain motionless. The snuffling got closer still. His heart hammered furiously in his throat. Finally, when he could hold his breath no longer, he gasped. A family of frightened raccoons scampered away. The tears he had been holding in for so long started to fall, pricking the corners of his eyes like hot needles.

"I'm trying to be brave," he said to the darkness. "I'm trying to be strong, but I'm all alone and I'm scared." He fingered the wolf's head pendant that hung around his neck. "Keep me safe," he prayed.

Suddenly he got an idea. He needed something sacred to make smoke. He didn't have tobacco or sage or sweetgrass, but he could smell cedar close by. Following his nose, he groped through the darkness and plucked some fresh fronds. Heading back to the glimmer of firelight, he carefully placed them on the dying embers and waited. At first he feared he had snuffed out the fire, but then smoke started to rise. He stretched his cupped hands into the rising plume and reverently washed the smoke over his head and shoulders as he had seen his people do so many times before. He couldn't remember the *Anishnaabemowin* words his parents and grandparents had used, so he made up his own prayer, hoping that Creator understood

English. "Great Spirit, watch over me and keep me safe."

Knowing that sacred smoke carried prayers to Creator, he crouched low to the ground and gently blew under the embers. The smoke rose in little billows and he flapped at it with his hands, sending it swirling upward. He spoke to the rising smoke. "Don't let that bad man catch me. Slow him down, turn him around. Confuse him."

He paused, knowing he was supposed to give thanks, but he couldn't find much in his situation to be thankful for. But then he remembered the old man who had helped him escape, the gifts of food that had sustained him, the matches that had lit his fire, and the rabbit-skin jacket that kept him warm. Then he gave thanks for the rabbits that had sacrificed their lives and given their furs, and for Crooked Ear, who wasn't with him right now but who he hoped was close by and would soon return.

Then he thought of Jesus, the school god, with long brown hair that flowed over his shoulders in the way of The People. George didn't have much confidence in Jesus. After all, the white men had killed him. If he was so powerful, why did he let them do that? However, the boy had found something likeable in the face of Jesus, who looked down at him from the walls of the chapel, the refectory, the classrooms, and the dormitory. George saw that Jesus had kindness in his eyes, even though those who said they loved him had hardness and cruelty in theirs.

So on this night, alone in the wilderness, George decided to pray to Jesus, too.

He cupped his hands again and respectfully offered the smoke into the air. Then he panicked.

Does smoke carry prayers to Jesus? At chapel they burn candles … they are not so smoky.

He waited for the smoke to die down to what he thought was just the perfect amount then started the school ritual, kneeling at the fireside, steepling his fingers and bowing his head.

"Jesus —" Deviating from the rote prayers, he spoke from his heart, spurred on by fear and desperation. "Help me. I know I am a just a filthy Indian, a good-for-nothing savage, but you are the Saviour, so save me from the bad man. And don't let the animals eat me."

He opened his eyes. The aurora borealis was swirling in the night sky, illuminating the lake in white light. He lay on his back and stared through the dream catcher to the sky. "And let the dream catcher work good so I don't get bad dreams."

The heavens shimmered and moved and he could not take his eyes from their hypnotic effect. His breath hovered briefly in front of his face then spiralled upward until it was swept away with the Northern Lights. Then, in the swirling eddies, wolves appeared. They loped across the sky, swooping down like birds, before rising up again. Once again the boy prayed, but this time to the wolves. "Keep me safe," he whispered.

The wolves came down to earth, encircling him, sitting on their haunches, forming a ring of protection. Their leader spoke, but not in words. His message entered the boy's consciousness as if by telepathy.

Close your eyes, Red Wolf. Sleep well. Know that we are guarding you. You are safe within our circle, little brother.

The boy slept peacefully.

In his dream, he looked into his father's eyes and he felt love cover him like a warm bearskin. Then HeWhoWhistles was gone, replaced by an image that George had seen every day at school: Jesus hanging on the cross. The God-man wore nothing but a breechcloth and a crown of sharp, twisted twigs tangled in his long brown hair. His eyes looked directly into George's. It was as if the dying God-man was seeing the real Red Wolf. Not 366. Not George. The God-man was seeing the soul of *Mishqua Ma'een'gun*.

He wanted to bask in the feeling forever, but he was whisked away and sent tumbling through the air until he found himself looking deep into the amber eyes of a wolf. The wolf wore Jesus's crown of twisted twigs, which even in the dream struck Red Wolf as more than a little strange.

Without words, the thoughts of the wolf flowed into the boy's soul.

When the strange ones came here, thinking they had discovered a new land, they did not see that wolves and true people had been here forever. There were no scratchy lines to say the land belonged to us and to the other creatures that fly, swim, crawl, or walk on four legs. We had no fences to keep us in, or them out. But you and I both know that from ocean to ocean, from mountaintop to river bottom, it was ours, together. Creator gave it to us, forever.

The strange ones took land that was not theirs to take, but no matter how much land they stole, they always wanted more. They were greedy and never satisfied.

They cut the trees that held life together for all of Creation.

They killed our prey, taking the furs but leaving the flesh to rot.

They put fences around the weak and stupid creatures they brought with them. Then, when we killed these stupid ones because our children were hungry, they called us ferocious savages and killed us with guns and poison.

They made reservations where the soil was weak and worthless, where there were no herds for hunting. And that was where they made your people live. And the laws made you stay there, a disinherited people forever.

In the name of God they stole you from your home and locked you behind walls where bad things happened. But they used the name of God falsely.

They say that their God is the true God, and that our Great Spirit is a deceiver. But it is they who are the deceivers. They made promises and treaties that they never intended to keep. Of all the promises they ever made, they kept only one; they promised to take our land and they did.

The boy was startled from sleep. A great blue heron soared over his head, her immense wings folding and twisting to carry her safely through the canopy. He looked at the mist hovering over the surface of the lake, heard the water lapping lazily against the rocks, and didn't know where he was. Then everything rushed into his mind. He looked for the circle of wolves. It wasn't there. He got up and searched the ground for tracks. There were plenty, unmistakably wolf: large pads, four toes, and non-retractable claws. They could have belonged to Crooked Ear, but faith told him they belonged to the heavenly wolves. He felt braver now. He felt protected, although he wished that Crooked Ear were with him.

Packing the dream catcher in his bag, he started down the trail and soon came to the shallow creek where he remembered resting with his father. Recalling what the old man had told him, he took off his boots and waded upstream, hoping to throw the dog off his scent. It was slow and painful progress on the humped and rounded stones. The dense spruces and cedars along the water's edge prevented the sun from filtering through, and soon he was chilled to the bone.

He climbed out on the far bank, and from that slightly elevated position he could see a beaver pond. Tree stumps stood around the shoreline, their tops nibbled into sharpened points like the pencils the boys used at school. A beaver lay on its back in the sunlit water, chewing on a small branch, but it rolled and dived as the boy lumbered clumsily toward it. He sat on a log in the sun, warming his ice-cold feet. He unwrapped his food, planning to eke out the meagre remains, but hunger got the better of him and he swallowed the bread and cheese in a single gulp.

A bittern walked furtively through the marsh grass, stalking its next meal. The bird plunged its head into the mud and when it came back up, the hind legs of a frog flailed from its beak. Tossing it in the air, the bird caught and swallowed it in one deft manoeuvre. The boy empathized with the frog.

Ravens cawing from a perch high above the landscape interrupted his thoughts. The raucous cries spoke to him, reminding him of his childhood, of his father and the ways of The People. The ravens said that an animal was dying, and that they were first in line. The final pieces of bread and cheese had left him feeling even hungrier than before, and he wondered if he could beat the ravens to the rabbit or bird whose life was coming to an end. He put his boots back onto his tingling feet and jogged off to investigate.

CHAPTER NINETEEN

The ravens looked down at the four-legged trapped in the snare. They bobbed their heads, watching keenly for signs of life, balancing hunger against the fear of approaching a living predator. One made a brief sortie, but when the trapped animal flailed its head and snarled, the bird quickly retreated to the treetop, landing clumsily alongside its companions, pitching them back and forth.

Suddenly their attention was diverted to the small Upright who had scrambled to the top of the rise, and with arms held out like wings was flying toward them, weaving in and out of the trees, all the while emitting a high-pitched, bird-like call. When he headed toward the dying animal, they attacked him. Red Wolf covered his head with his hands and ran.

A ferocious snarl stopped him dead in his tracks. Ahead, a wolf drew back his lips in a vicious grimace. The wolf looked so different from the animal he knew well that for a fleeting second the boy didn't recognize Crooked Ear.

"I'll get you out," he murmured, not knowing quite how and squatting a safe distance away to think. The wolf whimpered then licked and nibbled at the noose of snare wire that had all but disappeared into the swollen flesh of his front paw.

The boy traced the snare wire back to where it was secured to a metal peg embedded in the ground. He tugged, but it was anchored firmly and refused to give under his weight.

Crooked Ear was calm now, and the boy moved closer to get a better view. He stroked the big wolf's head and spoke gently. "I have to get that wire off. If I can loosen it, you'll be able to slip your paw out. Then you'll be free." Although he spoke the words with confidence, he was scared that pain would make the wolf attack him.

"It's going to hurt," he said, lightly touching the wolf's leg and slowly moving his fingers down to the injured paw. The animal flinched but didn't pull away. The boy spoke softly as he loosened the snare. Crooked Ear growled and flung his head toward the child, his fangs barely concealed behind grimacing lips. Red Wolf leapt out of the way.

Yelping in pain, the wolf pulled back his lips and delicately grasped the wire with his front teeth, teasing and loosening it until it lay harmless on the ground. Red Wolf, who had been watching so intently that he had barely drawn a breath, let out a gasp of relief. He wanted to throw his arms around the wolf and hug him, but he kept his distance, watching Crooked Ear gently lick the wound. Finally, with a heavy sigh, the wolf stretched out on his side, exhausted.

Red Wolf thought about the flat slabs of granite that sloped gently into Black Lake and wondered if Crooked Ear could get there and stand in the water to soothe his paw and drink. The boy remembered that it was not too far away, close to the stream that he had recently walked through.

He looked for the trail, but there was nothing but forest and bush. Panic rose in his throat. He ran back and forth, looking for any small sign from Mother Earth that he had passed that way. He collapsed at Crooked Ear's side and rested his head on the wolf's shoulder.

"We're lost," he said. "And I don't know how to help you. I'm sorry. I should have picked up Father's trail on the far side of the creek, but I walked *up*stream. I should have known that was wrong, especially when I reached the beaver pond, because when I made the trip with father we didn't pass a beaver pond! And then I followed the ravens, and I flew down the hill like a bird, forgetting to look around."

Scorn tainted his voice. "I was playing ... like a child!"

A voice spoke to his understanding. *If you had not done those things, you would not have found me, and I would have stayed in the trap until I died.*

The boy buried his face in the warmth of the wolf.

Crooked Ear struggled onto three legs and slowly limped into the bush. The boy followed, ducking under low boughs and using his hands to keep twigs and branches out of his face. The wolf's slow three-legged gait allowed him to keep up, and as long as they were together the boy felt calm. But after a while Crooked Ear broke into a hopping lope and vanished.

"Wait for me," Red Wolf pleaded in panic. He forced himself to calm down and do what HeWhoWhistles would do: he searched for paw tracks, snapped twigs, bruised leaves. Slowly he followed the wolf's trail through the dense forest. Suddenly blue sky greeted him and great slabs of granite sloped toward Black Lake. Crooked Ear was standing in the water, drinking. The boy felt a wave of relief.

Even when he raised his head, Crooked Ear remained in the water. Meanwhile, Red Wolf searched for a strong stick and sharpened it to a point. In quick succession he speared three fish. He tossed two to Crooked Ear, who swallowed them whole, but he cooked his fish over a fire.

Red Wolf didn't notice in the disappearing light that grey clouds had gathered. He curled up close to the fire, the rabbit skin jacket covering him from head to toe. Crooked Ear limped in three tight circles and flopped down beside him. He licked his paw a few more times then tucked his nose into his chest, wrapped his thick bushy tail around his body, and went to sleep.

Not long after dawn, Red Wolf was awakened by the complaint of a chickadee that plumped up its feathers against the brisk air. Red Wolf sat up, surprised when a light dusting of snow slid from him. He looked for Crooked Ear, but the wolf was gone. He called out urgently, and a black-tipped nose poked out from under the snow. Crooked Ear heaved himself up and made a half-hearted attempt to shake before flopping down and lethargically licking his wounded leg.

Red Wolf was dismayed. The leg was swollen to twice its normal size. Anxiety tensed his stomach into a knot. He looked at the sky. Light snow swirled through the treetops and he shivered. *I must get home … the weather is getting bad … I have no food. But Crooked Ear can't walk! If I go without him, what will become of him? I can't leave him.*

He rebuilt the fire and sat by it until his shivering stopped. He speared more fish and held one under Crooked Ear's nose, but the wolf wouldn't eat. He tried to build a shelter, but cutting through the spruce boughs was too difficult. He crawled under the low-lying branches of a dense stand of cedars. The thick foliage kept most of the snow from the ground, and it smelled good. Crooked Ear limped after the boy. The child gently stroked the wolf's head. His nose was hot. The boy knew that fever often killed children. He presumed it killed wolves, too.

He fingered his pendant and prayed to the spirit wolves he hoped were still guarding him. "Help us, please."

He didn't know what else to do.

CHAPTER TWENTY

The Indian agent had lost a lot of time by diverting into town and riling up the farmers with his story of child-eating wolves. Crooked Ear was, of course, the primary target of his revenge, but by the time the effect of the poison bait rippled through the environment, the wolf was long gone. The Indian agent didn't waste any emotion on other wild animals that he knew would feed on the bait: bears, foxes, raccoons, martens, and wolverines. These animals were disposable as far as he was concerned, so he spared no thought for them or their abandoned offspring. Had he realized that birds such as ravens, vultures, crows, jays, and owls would also die when they fed on poisoned carcasses, he would not have cared much either. As long as the woodlands continued to harbour game animals such as deer, elk, and rabbits he was happy. He had no knowledge that rain and melting snow would carry poison into the streams, rivers, ponds, and lakes, contaminating the fish and waterbirds he enjoyed on his dinner plate from time to time.

The Indian agent was focused on one thing alone: catching 366. He cantered, hoping to catch up before the trail went cold. He sensed a shift in the wind and looked up. Clouds scudded from the north. It was not a good sign and he knew it would be wise to turn around and head home. If he got caught in an early snowstorm, the footing would be difficult and the going slow. It would be sensible to let the Mounties pick up the boy from the reserve when the weather improved.

He reined in the gelding and called to the dog, but the animal was snuffling through the dirt and vegetation fifty yards ahead, and ignored his master's command. The dog had picked up a fresh scent! Excitement coursed through the Indian agent and a sadistic grin lit his face. "So, Horse Thief, you're close by, eh?"

His joints were stiff with cold, and when he dismounted his feet hit the ground like two bricks, sending a jolt right through him, but he was elated. He kicked at the remains of the boy's fire to see if there were any glowing embers. A look of satisfaction spread over his face; he wasn't far behind. He cast around for any sign of wolves, fear tugging at his gut, although with his rifle slung over his shoulder, he felt braver. The only paw prints he saw were from his dog. The animal had trampled the area in his excitement, inhaling the feral smells that encircled the boy's bed.

A few minutes earlier the agent had been ready to turn for home, but sensing that he was within striking range, he wanted to press on. However, the light was fading. It would soon be dark. He decided to make camp and catch the boy in the morning.

The Northern lights danced again across the night sky, but neither the Indian agent nor his quarry a few miles along the trail saw the shimmering green curtains of heaven.

In the cedar bower at the edge of Black Lake, Crooked Ear's feverish heat warmed the boy. The wolf whimpered in his sleep, his paws twitching. At one point he howled, but the boy, sleeping under the dream catcher, didn't stir.

Red Wolf was a baby again. His father held him up to the heavens to be blessed by the spirits.

"Creator, thank you for this boy child who has completed my life," He Who Whistles said. "Spirit of the red wolf, watch over my son. He shares your name. Let him also share your speed and grace, your honour and courage, your strength and compassion."

Then Red Wolf was wrenched from his father's hands and whisked into the air like a dry leaf in an autumn storm. He tumbled through space until he came face-to-face with a wise and serene wolf.

"The time has come, little brother. You must run now, like never before. I will stay with you."

The child felt himself changing. He was on all fours, marvelling at his sleek red coat and bushy tail. Then, surrounded by wolves from snow-white to black and through all the shades of brown, red, and grey, he found himself running. He was fast and powerful, graceful and courageous. Pride welled inside him like a spring, bubbling up from the earth. But most important of all, he was free.

When he awoke at daybreak, he felt more like Red Wolf, less like George, definitely not like 366. He poked his head from under the cedar fronds and saw Venus, the morning star for whom his mother had been named, still glimmering in the dawn sky. It was a sign, he thought. Crooked Ear had already nosed his way out of the cedars and was helping himself to the remainder of the fish, licking up the last scales and bones from the ground. The boy was hungry, but he was glad, at least, that the wolf had a good appetite. It meant that he was healing.

"I hope you can run today," he said. "We must get home before the blizzards come." Crooked Ear seemed to understand, and with barely a limp he trotted forward. The boy gathered up his bag, put on his boots, and chased after the wolf.

Back down the trail, the Indian agent was not happy. There was an icy chill in the morning air and he couldn't get warm. He had spent a restless night trying to fit his body around the bumps on the cold ground. When he had heard the howl of a lone wolf, he sat upright and grabbed his gun. His hands were so cold he could barely feel the trigger. After that, every rustle in the bush brought a renewed surge of panic that loosened his bowels and sent him scurrying outside the tent, gun in hand, trousers around his ankles.

His courage returned along with the daylight. He tossed grain for the hobbled horse, and with his gut telling him the boy was just a few miles ahead, he was soon back on the trail. When they reached the creek, the dog could find no scent. The animal ran up and down on both banks without success. The Indian agent, however, could see a faint path on the far bank. He turned his horse toward the creek and dug in his heels. The horse balked. The man's temper rose and he leaned out of the saddle to snap a slender branch from a tree. Squaring the horse to the creek, he gave him a whack on his rear end and the animal threw himself across the water.

When they reached Black Lake, the dog ran along the sloping black rocks until he found the boy's campsite in the cedar bower. The agent held his hand over the ashes and felt a trace of warmth. Horse Thief was close.

He heard a splash. Brown lake trout were jumping through the clear water. The thought of fried fish made his mouth water and overrode his urge to catch the boy. He took his fishing gear from the saddlebags and cast into the lake. Almost immediately a fish was on the line. He ripped the hook from its gaping mouth and left it to flounder on the rocks, turning his attention to the remains of the boy's fire. The charcoal re-ignited easily, and soon the fire was blazing.

He hadn't noticed the pair of ravens on a nearby tree. They were unusually quiet. One of the birds swooped down, grabbed the fish in its beak, and struggled to lift itself back into the air.

"Hey! You miserable buzzard!" the agent shouted. "That's my breakfast!"

He lunged at the raven, but his feet slipped on the damp rocks and he sprawled face first.

Within a few laboured wing-beats the raven dropped the heavy fish. It slapped onto the granite. Optimistic that breakfast was yet again within his grasp, the agent scrambled toward it, but he was thwarted. The second raven swooped down and carried the fish away. The man cursed and threw stones. Enraged, he barely noticed the ice pellets stinging his upturned face.

The first raven circled back. It was coincidence that the bird voided just as it flew overhead.

For the Indian agent it was the last straw. Spitting and spluttering in disgust, he kicked dirt over the fire, climbed on his horse, and headed home.

CHAPTER TWENTY-ONE

Freezing rain encased the naked branches of the trees and icicles clung to the guard hairs of Crooked Ear's coat. The smell of wood smoke reached the wolf's nose long before the boy's. A few more minutes and they both saw it curling from the chimneys of shacks and cabins. Away from the cover of the trees the ground was slick, and coupled with his haste to reach his parents' cabin, Red Wolf slipped and fell several times. But at last he threw open the door. A rush of smoky warm air hit him. His parents looked up in surprise, then they were both talking at the same time, both trying to hug him and feed him.

All too quickly their excitement and delight turned to concern.

"They will come for you! They will take you back!" HeWhoWhistles said, his voice pitched with stress.

The child cringed. He saw himself tied to the post at school, flinching as the whip cut into his back. He had been right; his mother and father couldn't protect him. They would send him back.

"We can leave the reserve," he said, searching for the right *Anishnaabemowin* words and stringing them together as fast as he could, desperate to say these things before his enthusiasm was tainted by the hopelessness he read on his parents' faces.

"We can live in a *wiigwam*, as we did in the old times. We can hunt and trap and fish. We can eat berries and nuts and —"

"The big snows are coming," HeWhoWhistles interrupted.

Red Wolf felt as if he had been thrown into a raging river. He was being pulled under by the weight of drenched clothes.

"If the snows are big enough they won't come for me," he murmured, phrasing it neither as a question nor a fact, but a fervent wish that might stop him from drowning.

"We can hope," HeWhoWhistles replied, already longing for the life his son was suggesting, but weighing the difficulties born of maturity. "We have no supplies ready, son. We need toboggans, snowshoes, strong shelter, warm clothes, food. It will take time to prepare. If we go now, unprepared, we will die...."

The unfamiliar words droned on and on, leaving Red Wolf in a blur of incomprehension. But at school he had learned to read faces and body language; he knew that his father was giving valid reasons for not leaving the reserve immediately.

"If we go without passes, they will chase us down and throw us in the place we cannot get out of. Our only choice is to go far away, to the north where they will not follow."

HeWhoWhistles paused to think. *Is there a place where the pale-faced ones will not follow?* His voice took on a tone of resignation. "We cannot leave now. We must prepare. We will go in spring."

The boy understood, and his heart sank even lower. *What if they come for me before spring?*

Later, when Red Wolf slept and Crooked Ear lay curled up against the outside wall of the cabin, HeWhoWhistles paced the wooden floor, searching for a solution, but he could not find one.

I was deceived. I brought my family to this place of misery and captivity. My woman weaves mats and baskets, and sews coloured beads on moccasins to trade with the white man for firewater. His thoughts brought a sneer to his lips.

Our son is not ours anymore. Our daughter... she will be taken from us, just as Mishqua Ma'een'gun *was taken.*

They have fire-sticks. They have places that a man cannot get out of.

I cannot protect my woman and my children.

I wish I could go back in time and choose a different path. I would go north with my brothers and live Anishnaabek Bemazawin, *the True Life, just as*

189

in the old days. I would teach my children to live the natural way. We would know hunger. It would be hard. But I would be a man and we would be together.

The elk and moose and deer have gone away from here. They do not wish to live close to the white ones who show no kindness or respect.

He sighed deeply.

We cannot leave this place unless they say we can. They give scraps of paper to say when to go and when to come back. Who are they to say such things? He lowered his head into his hands. *The snow has come early. Maybe it will melt before winter sets in hard. Then the men will come on horses and take my son.* He prayed that the snow would stay, that it would worsen and lie deep on the ground. With daylight he would search for a place to hide Red Wolf for the winter. He would find a cave or build a shelter deep in the woods. In spring they would all leave the reserve together.

The black horses were lathered in sweat, their recently acquired winter coats too warm for the unseasonably mild November day. The men had already shed their waterproof capes and furs, bundling them behind the British Cavalry saddles and, as the midday sun intensified, they unbuttoned their scarlet Norfolk coats, too.

As they approached Anishnaabe territory, they checked the readiness of their weapons. The sergeant didn't anticipate any problems finding or identifying the boy; he would be the only school-age child on the reserve. But past experience had shown him that the natives could behave with irrational savagery. He was not going to take any chances with the lives of his men. They re-buttoned their jackets and trotted onto the reserve, the lead rider bearing a lance, the sergeant and other soldiers riding in single file on the narrow trail.

Crooked Ear smelled them long before they reached the area where the cabins, shacks, and *wiigwams* stood. He whined at the boy and nudged his hands. Red Wolf was in tune with the animal's body language and realized at once he was in danger. He looked around but saw nothing. Crooked Ear whined again and trotted off into the bush and the child followed, but it was too late. The lead rider had caught sight of him running into the distance. The sergeant shouted the order and the horses broke into a gallop.

Red Wolf ran as fast as he could, trying to reach the deep forest where he knew the low hanging branches would hamper the progress of the horses. The sound of pounding hooves grew louder and louder. He pumped his legs as hard as they would go, ducking under the first tree limb, scrambling over fallen logs and swatting branches from his face.

The hoofbeats stopped, but someone was chasing him on foot. Red Wolf was already fatigued. The policeman was fresh. The boy tripped over a root, and before he could scramble to his feet, a massive leather boot stomped down on his upper back, pushing his face into the dirt. He struggled with all his remaining strength to rise, but his arms were wrenched behind his back and his hands were tied. Exhausted, he allowed himself to be led back to his parents' cabin.

StarWoman could not bear to watch. She snatched the hand of her young daughter and ran in the opposite direction, as far and as fast as she could, deep into the bush. She didn't return until nightfall.

HeWhoWhistles remained, an 1876 Winchester pointed at his chest. He watched the police tie Red Wolf to the saddle, and he searched for words to tell his son that he blamed himself for what was happening, that he despised himself for his weakness, that he wished with all his heart that he could go back in time and make things right. But his dark eyes were damp with tears and the words stuck in his throat.

From the back of the horse, Red Wolf looked into his father's face and was angry. Hatred surged into his throat like vomit; hatred for HeWhoWhistles for not being all-powerful, hatred for StarWoman for not being there. He hated them both for not loving him enough to fight for him. He fought back his tears and said nothing.

On the narrow trail, the horses picked up the pace, keen to be heading home. Occasionally they tensed, pricked their ears, and snorted restlessly, sensing that danger was close. The riders glanced around, but they didn't see the wolf following at a distance.

As darkness fell, the boy heard a lonely howl and he knew that Crooked Ear, at least, was missing him.

CHAPTER TWENTY-TWO

George was fortunate. Father Thomas had reflected upon Turtle's overly severe punishment and had restricted Mister Hall's whippings to ten lashes. George was tied to the courtyard post by his wrists and all the students were made to gather around and watch. The knotted rawhide whip ripped into the flesh of his back and coiled around his ribcage. George didn't make a sound. And at the very end Henry started to stomp his boot on the ground. Others picked up the rhythm, until George felt the ground pulsing like a drum. Mister Hall was livid. He shouted himself hoarse.

George didn't know that the entire student body went to bed that night without supper. He was in the infirmary. He didn't cry as the nurse washed and packed salve into the lacerations, or as she wrapped him in bandages.

After his recovery George realized that his position in the schoolboy pecking order had changed. Boys no longer tormented him, and even Henry behaved differently, his taunts seemingly more for show. Under different circumstances the two boys might have become friends, but George's anger seethed inside as if a fire burned in his chest. His rage was not compatible with friendship.

After a fresh snowfall, when the barbs of the fence were piled high with soft white cones, an illusion of peace blanketed the school. A passerby would never have suspected the despair contained within the walls. But the winter months at Bruce County School were the hardest months of all. No matter how bad the weather, animals still had to be fed and mucked out, snow had to be shovelled, firewood had to be chopped, and stoves kept burning. Despite their non-stop efforts to heat the building, the dormitories were so cold that the boys' breath lingered in front of their faces, condensing on the windowpanes, and freezing overnight into delicate crystalline ferns that swirled across the glass.

With winter came sickness and death, but as much as Red Wolf would have welcomed death, he continued living, day by awful day; days that finally warmed and lengthened until June came to an end, and once again he waited by the window with the other boys, an ember of hope flaring in his chest. He tried to extinguish the little flame but it refused to die.

He waited and waited but his father never came.

No tears trickled down his cheeks. He felt no loss or sorrow, but his anger burned behind cold, impassive features. The next day Father Thomas escorted George to his office. There was no pre-amble, nothing to prepare the boy for the shock that was to come. Father Thomas spoke the words in the same matter-of-fact tone that he used to announce the day of the week.

"Your father has been hanged."

"What is hanged?" George asked.

The priest thought for a few moments, search-ing for the right words to describe this European punishment. He didn't approve of capital punish-ment and found hanging to be rather barbaric.

"Never mind, George. Suffice to say, your father is dead."

George gasped.

The priest placed his hand compassionately on the boy's shoulder. "I am your only father now. You'll stay here over the summer vacation and work for local farmers who need extra help."

Father Thomas's voice droned on, his hand heavy on the boy's shoulder. George felt it weigh-ing him down, as if he were being crushed into the ground. The priest pulled away and rustled through the papers on his desk until he found what he was looking for.

"It says here that your mother has turned to alcohol and that nothing can be done for her."

He tutted disparagingly. "It's the devil's firewater for sure. You will not be allowed to return to her. It's for your own protection, George. She could hurt you."

The child watched the priest's mouth open and close like a fish left on the rocks. "Your sister has been taken away from her, too. She's been put up for adoption. Oh, that's excellent news. She'll have a much better life that way. "

The boy's throat went dry and he watched Father Thomas recede into a long, dark tunnel lit by twinkling stars. White light bounced off the two circles of glass that balanced in front of the priest's eyes. The child swayed. And everything went black.

When he regained consciousness, he was a changed person. Until then, he had fleetingly and intermittently believed that he was still *Mishqua Ma'een'gun*. Despite the shocking things he had learned about The People, their powerlessness to stand firm against the white man, and his anger toward his family for abandoning him, he still sometimes thought of himself as Red Wolf. He thought of himself as George, too, but never as 366. But when he learned that his father was dead and his mother cared more for the devil's firewater than for him, he became George, 366. It brought stillness to his spirit. There was no more inner conflict, no turmoil. He was numb. He was dumb. He was George.

George was never told the whole story surrounding his father's violent death. He thought once again that the teachers were right. Indians were savages, drunks, good-for-nothings.

CHAPTER TWENTY-THREE

Crooked Ear's bond to the boy was strong. Each summer he passed through the place where meadow had once met forest. He lingered briefly, his powerful nose searching through the man smells for any scent of the boy, but there was none.

Much had changed since his first visit. The wild flowers that had randomly poked their delicate heads above meadow grasses were gone, replaced by straight rows of corn. Rails of cedar zigzagged around pastures dotted with stumps of forest giants.

He watched four-leggeds standing in the enclosures with their young ones. The creatures were not elk, deer, or moose on which wolves normally preyed, but Crooked Ear's keen sense of smell told him that the young ones would make a tasty meal. Saliva dripped from his mouth. He lowered his body to the ground and started to advance. But as he got closer, the rank odour of Uprights alerted him and he moved on.

He visited the reserve where his Upright had once lived. The boy was not there. There were dogs for companionship, but The People were not keen to have him in their midst, so he slunk away, moving south toward Clear Lake. The landmarks of old trees were gone and he became disoriented. He sniffed at the stumps, rubbing his neck against the rough-sawn fibres and lifting his leg to leave his mark. He moved on, reaching what he knew to be a wide river, but it was so full of logs that it looked as solid as land. On the opposite bank a team of heavy horses fussed while Uprights struggled to roll the logs into the flow.

Crooked Ear ran on in panic, slithering to a stop when he saw two Uprights ahead. They were pushing and pulling a huge double saw across the trunk of a massive tree. Crooked Ear backed up on silent pads.

A sound of creaking came from the treetops. The Uprights stopped grunting and turned their eyes upward. For a moment all was still and silent. Then they ran.

"Timber!"

The big tree moved, almost imperceptibly at first. The strong trunk fibres that had not been severed by the saw twisted, popped, and ripped, losing their battle to hold the tree upright. It crashed to the ground, shaking the earth beneath Crooked Ear's pads. He fled and didn't look back.

After the initial burst of speed, the wolf settled into a lope that took him north, well away from human habitation, into territory he had never crossed before. For the duration of the waxing moon he ran. When he finally came upon fresh lupine odour, he threw back his head and yipped in elation.

The following night his howls were answered. The replies were mostly deep in tone, warning him that he was inside the territory of others, but Crooked Ear so craved lupine contact that he was more than prepared to risk the pack's rejection. Within minutes he galloped the final mile and slithered to a stop in front of a wall of wolves. They stood aloof, tails high but still, their body language saying that the newcomer was not welcome.

The alpha male raised his hackles and growled. Instantly Crooked Ear bowed to the ground. With his haunches pointed to the sky, he wagged his tail and whined like a pup. The wolves did not react, so Crooked Ear advanced a few paces, keeping his front legs and chest low to the ground. Again there was no reaction. Finally he rolled onto his back and lay perfectly still. The alpha male decided that Crooked Ear was harmless and allowed him into the pack.

Over the summer moons Crooked Ear hunted with the Great Northern Wolf Pack, learning skills that Tall-Legs and Tika had not had time to teach him and refining those that he had picked up from Seraph and the pack at Clear Lake. He was a brave and intelligent hunter. As a result he quickly moved up the hierarchy of the pack and was allowed to feed alongside the others at the kill. He had also filled out. He now had the height that came from Tall-Legs and the girth that came from Tika. He was striking in appearance, his burnished red coat so different from the mottled shades of grey, brown, and black of the other wolves. He was in his prime but had no desire to challenge the alpha for the leadership of the pack. Because of this, Crooked Ear was forced to remain without a mate, as pack rules dictated.

As the days grew shorter, Crooked Ear became restless. He had searched long and hard to find a pack that would accept him, and yet he yearned to leave. Something was missing in his life. It could have been a mate, it could have been the little Upright, or merely a homing instinct, but whatever it was his pads led the way, and without conscious thought, Crooked Ear found himself on the long journey back to Clear Lake, to the den sheltered under the ridge where he was born.

He repeated this journey year after year, but when the sun was highest in the sky he always waited at the place where the forest had once met the meadow — until the time he crested the ridge at Clear Lake and saw man-dens at the edge of the water. The scent of Seraph and the others lingered on the trees and boulders and in the soil, but none of the smells was recent. Crooked Ear knew that the pack had moved far away. He had no strength left in his tired limbs to follow. He turned and with head and tail low wandered back into the forest.

CHAPTER TWENTY-FOUR

George's formal education ended with Grade Eight graduation. The ceremony was held in the school dining room and officiated by Father Thomas. The whole student body was there, as well as the staff, but no family or friends. The graduating boys didn't mind. Most of them had lost touch with their families.

Father Thomas thanked God profusely for bringing so many heathen children into the Christian family and for eliminating the Indian problem by assimilating them into civilized society. He prayed for the souls of the little ones who had been lost along the way, those who had not made it to graduation. George remembered Turtle. He hadn't thought of his friend for a long time. He tried to see an image of the boy in his mind's eye, or hear his voice, but when he squeezed his eyes shut all he saw was bursts of bright light, like flashing stars in a deep purple sky. Turtle was gone. George could remember no more than his name and the fact that once, a very long time ago, they were friends, best friends; in fact, Turtle was his one and only friend.

Father Thomas droned on while George contemplated that only eight boys from the original thirty in his Grade One class were graduating. Most of the missing boys were in the cemetery behind the school. George remembered that he used to fantasize that the dead boys had escaped and were once again living with their mothers and fathers, brothers and sisters, and extended families. He was seven or eight when he put such childish thoughts behind him.

He was jolted from his reverie by a chorus of monotone voices chanting *Aaah-men*. And then Father Thomas, with a broad smile on his face, led the students in a round of applause to congratulate the graduates. Applause was not part of regular school life. It was even rarer than the smile on Father Thomas's face, so the boys clapped until their palms were red and tingling. With this, George officially moved on to the next stage of his life: two more years at Bruce County Indian Residential School, the only difference being that instead of classes in the morning and farm work in the afternoon, it would now be farm work all day long. But it suited George well. He worked mostly without supervision. As long as he did his job well, there was no punishment.

Dawn milking was George's favourite chore. It was quiet in the barn, no angry voices or shouted commands, no whacks of the cane, just the cows chewing the cud. He leaned his forehead against the flank of the cow, watching each squirt of milk turn to froth, making music by aiming the flow to the side of the pail. The repetitive sound calmed him, resonating with a rhythm that seemed to be part of his soul; a drumming, reminiscent of a heartbeat.

Henry and George had come to an understanding, too. Henry had changed, softened. The transformation had happened soon after Master Evans left the school. At the time George did not see the connection. He had always felt uncomfortable around Master Evans, despite the fact that the Grade One teacher was kinder than most of the staff. But a day came when suddenly George knew the truth. He remembered the look on Top Boy Frank's face when Henry had come across the field all those years ago. Back then George couldn't understand why Frank would feel sorry for Henry. But now he found himself looking at Henry with that same expression, and he was astounded that he had been so blind.

George never raised the subject of abuse with Henry, and Henry never volunteered any information, but now George understood what Henry had endured. And Henry knew that George knew. The shared secret was enough to bring peace to the previously turbulent relationship between the two boys.

There was no doubt that Henry was the best chicken killer in the school. He would hold the bird by its feet, slam it onto the old maple stump, anchor it with his boot, and wait until all the senior boys were watching him. Then he would raise the axe and with one swift movement lop the squawking head clean off.

Then came the moment the boys had been waiting for; Henry moved his boot. The headless chicken flapped its wings, leapt upwards from the maple stump, landed on its yellow feet, and high-stepped around the yard. The boys shrieked and shoved each other to get the best possible view while dodging the hapless chicken and the gushing blood. In unison they counted.

"One … and … two … and … three … and …"

George never wanted to take part in the ritual, but he did, his eyes drawn to the macabre sight as though he had no control of them. Despite his aversion, he behaved as enthusiastically as the others, pushing, betting, fitting in, surviving.

"Look, the stupid bird doesn't know it's dead," Henry often shrieked, doubling over in gales of laughter.

Words of The People would form in George's head. He didn't recognize the male voice that spoke them. And he had retained no understanding of

Anishnaabemowin, but as the headless chickens ran around the farmyard, the strange phrase echoed through his head, and stranger still, he knew what the words meant.

I am not yet dead, but already I am in hell!

George knew that it applied to more than the headless chicken.

When the headless bird finally crumpled to the ground, twitched and lay still, there was always an uproar, the boys arguing about who had won.

The stronger boys pushed the weaker ones until a winner was declared. Then the losers pushed each other around some more, trying to decide how to divide the winner's chores.

George hated both killing and gutting chickens. The metallic smell of blood and the slick feel of guts in his hands turned his stomach. But he didn't mind the time-consuming job of plucking feathers, so Henry killed and gutted, and George plucked. Henry, however, who was always so amused by the headless chickens, and who would unravel intestines with glee, would clutch his groin protectively at the prospect of castrating piglets. That job fell to George.

Both boys understood that male piglets had to be castrated. The boar that was kept for breeding purposes was evidence that uncastrated piglets grew into dangerous, unmanageable animals. George knew that the strength and wildness that he took from a piglet had been taken from him too, albeit in a different manner. Like the pigs, he had become docile, domesticated, and tame.

George had been called *savage* almost every day of his school life. With the help of the pigs he learned that the opposite of *savage* was not *obedient*, or *well-behaved*, or *educated*, as he had been led to believe. The opposite of *savage* was *tame*. George felt a stab in his chest when he realized that the word described him well.

A year after graduation, Henry came out of Father Thomas's office yelling that he was finally free to leave. George shared his excitement but was saddened by the news. He was going to miss Henry. Hurriedly, the two boys promised to look each other up in the outside world when they both had jobs and homes of their own. Then Henry was gone.

George didn't know how much longer he would have to wait for his day of freedom. He didn't know when his fifteenth birthday was. He had been given an official birthdate for the school record, but neither this date nor his real birth date had ever been celebrated. The children marked the passage of time by grades, not birthdays, thinking of themselves as Grade One, or Grade Three, or Grade Eight. After graduation, George was gradeless. So it came as a surprise when, the year after Henry left, Father Thomas summoned George to the office and told him he could leave. He didn't have to wait until the end of the year, the end of the term, or even the end of the day!

George had longed for this day for ten years, but as Father Thomas unlocked the gate, he was filled with trepidation. The priest pressed a few coins into his hand and ushered him to the outside world.

"This will help you get through the first few days, until you get on your feet."

George had never had money of his own and wondered what he might buy with it.

"It won't go far," the priest warned. "You need to find a job. Soon. Understand?"

The gate slammed behind him. Rust flakes rained down onto the small suitcase that contained all his worldly possessions. George looked up to the orange strand of barbed wire that coiled along the top of the gate and remembered that once he had tried to scale it. It had seemed so high then. Now he could stretch up and touch it if he wanted to.

Father Thomas turned the key in the lock. The metallic clunk reminded George of something, although at first he couldn't quite remember what it was. Then an image flashed across his inner eye: a man on his knees, clutching the gate, wailing. George didn't like what he saw. He didn't like the weakness that he perceived in the man's tears. He didn't like the turmoil that was stirring inside his chest. He wanted to be back on the other side of the gate, where he had no feelings, where he had a bed to sleep in, food to eat, and where he was told what to do and when to do it, where he didn't have to look after himself. He almost pleaded with the Father to let him back in, but ten years had taught him not to speak unless spoken to. He remained mute and watched the priest walk away.

George was alone.

Accustomed to following orders, he did exactly what Father Thomas had suggested. He headed toward town to get a job. His confidence rose as he walked. He imagined working in the general store, stocking the shelves, loading supplies into horse-drawn wagons, maybe even steadying the horses, or serving the customers. He saw himself living on Main Street in a house with curtains in the windows and paint on the door.

The shopkeeper told George that he never hired Injuns. "Not that I object to your kind, myself," he said. "It's the customers, see. They won't stand for it. They won't tolerate your dirty hands touching the produce."

George looked at his hands. They were indeed a little dirty from the walk to town. "I can wash them, sir."

The shopkeeper laughed and escorted George from the store. "I'm sorry, boy, but I can't afford to lose any customers."

The feed store owner shooed George away as though he was one of the flea-ridden cats that lived off mice in the mill. "Don't come back unless you want to *buy* something."

And the blacksmith said he would never take on an Indian as an apprentice.

George wanted to get out of town as fast as he could. He walked past the picket fences and painted front doors of Main Street, his head down, his eyes averted from the staring eyes of the towns-folk. During the years at Bruce County Indian Residential School, George had been repeatedly told that education and assimilation would secure his future, but in his heart he always suspected he would never be educated enough, never assimilated enough, never good enough, never white enough. Now he knew for sure.

He headed into the countryside, following Father Thomas's final instruction. It was almost dark and he had no place to sleep and no supper to eat, but he was optimistic, knowing that he would far rather milk cows on a farm than serve white folk in a store. He was more comfortable with animals than with people. Animals didn't lie. Animals didn't hurt you as long as you didn't hurt them.

That night George slept as an uninvited guest in a derelict barn, and the next day he worked at the only job he could get: shovelling manure. Acceptance of his low status came naturally. Working knee-deep in manure was what he had been trained for, what he deserved.

CHAPTER TWENTY-FIVE

Bill Clark didn't much like the idea of hiring an Indian, but he'd been unable to shake off the cough that had plagued him since the previous winter, and he was feeling low. He needed help and the Indian was the cheapest labourer he could find. George planted, weeded, harvested, hayed, mended fences, and shovelled manure, and he did it all without complaint. What's more, the old farmer noticed that his Clydesdale liked George. Her affection toward the boy was a good recommendation.

Daisy was the biggest animal George had ever seen. Her withers were higher than his head, and he couldn't see the top of her back. But once he got over the shock of her immense size and strength, he realized that she was a gentle and sweet-natured creature with no trace of malice. He felt safer around her than he did around white folk because he sensed she wouldn't try to hurt him. Most white folk, on the other hand, made his heart beat fast, his stomach churn, and sweat break out on the palms of his hands.

Bill Clark had not intended to let George work with Daisy. He never let the hired hands touch his precious horse. George was to do everything else, leaving Bill the time and energy to see to Daisy, but when the farmer brought the Clydesdale back to the barn after a hard morning in the field, George pumped water from the well so that the horse could drink. That pleased Bill. It showed him that the boy cared about the horse. He reasoned that if he taught the boy how to unharness Daisy, brush her down, and feed her, he could take his weary self to the farmhouse and lie down for a bit.

The farmer set about teaching his young protégé how to care for Daisy. "There's no point in trying to force your will on her," he said. "If it comes to strength she'll win. She's got to trust you enough to let you be the boss. Once she knows what you want, she'll be happy to oblige. She'll do just about anything to please you."

George was a quick learner and soon Daisy was willingly dropping her head into the bridle to take the iron bit from his hand, and picking up her enormous feathered feet so that he could clean the dirt from her hooves.

The first time George led Daisy out of the barn alone, when she clopped alongside him to the drive-shed and backed into the traces of the plough, he felt something warm in his chest. He was disappointed when the farmer refused to teach him to drive the horse. George had to be content with watching the rapport between the old man and his horse, spotting the barely perceptible touch of the long reins that controlled the mare's every footfall. He watched the pair cultivate the soil, working together as a team, and he imagined himself behind the horse, steadying the ploughshare, feeling the reins, encouraging Daisy forward with the cluck of his tongue.

When the day's work was done and the horse was standing knee-deep in a bed of fresh straw, George would unlatch the stall door and go in with her. He didn't talk to her aloud in the English words that were his only language. He talked to her with his thoughts. And sometimes he felt that she talked back.

"Boss, you don't look too good today," George said, noticing the sallow hue to the old man's weathered skin.

"I'm fine," Bill Clark replied with a cough and a wheeze. "I aim to plough the south field today and tomorrow, then get it harrowed —"

"I can do it, boss," George interrupted.

Bill Clark guffawed, which brought on a fresh spell of coughing. "Lad, it takes years to learn to plough a field," he said once the spasm had passed.

"I know how, boss! I've been watching you good. Me and Daisy could plough a straight line, for sure."

"It's not as easy as it looks, boy. But you're right. I don't feel too good today, so go harness the horse and let's see what you can do. If you make a right mess of it, no harm done. I'll just do it over."

Almost by instinct, it seemed, George was able to guide Daisy down the edge of the furrow, angling the plough, its sharp edge cutting deep into the soil. He quickly learned to balance the speed of the horse with the tilt of the ploughshare so that a wave of fresh, damp earth ran continuously from the blade, settling behind him in an almost straight line. Within a day he was a master. Within three days the job was done. He took satisfaction from the symmetry of the ploughed field, and he could have stared at its beauty forever. It hurt him a little when the farmer told him to harness the horse to the drag harrow and make that first pass over the immaculately ploughed field. His thoughts wandered to the intricate frosty designs on the dormitory windows and to Mother Hall, who always made them scrape it off. He hated destroying a thing of beauty then, and he hated it now.

But to his surprise, harrowing the field brought fresh satisfaction. With his job complete, he leaned his head against Daisy's shoulder and gazed over the tilled field, inhaling the earthy smell that mingled with horse sweat. He stooped to pick up a handful of crumbly soil and let it run through his fingers. It gave him a sense of well-being that was normally absent from his life. He remembered how he felt at school when he milked the cows, and deep down inside he knew that he could be more than a hired hand. He knew he could be a farmer. Desire rose in his throat, the yearning for his own land, a horse like Daisy, perhaps a few cows, some pigs, and chickens. But how could he be a farmer when he had no land and when he had no money to buy machinery or livestock? He pushed the longing back down. It could never happen. It was a crazy thought. No, he would stay here on Mr. Clark's farm. The job suited him. Life was good.

As winter settled in, George shivered under his blanket in the hayloft. Bill Clark gave him some winter clothes that had once belonged to his son, and a pile of old blankets, and told him to come up to the farmhouse and warm himself by the wood stove. "You chopped the wood, lad, you may as well warm yourself with it." But George never went. He was not accustomed to being toasty warm in winter. He preferred to go into Daisy's stall. The heat from her enormous body kept him warm enough.

The morning that Bill found Daisy and George asleep together in the straw, the old farmer made a decision that was surprising even to him.

"George," he said when the young man stirred, "I'm going to leave that horse to you in my will."

George had no understanding of what a will was, and Bill had to explain. George was speechless.

The old man then spoke the longest sentence of his life. "Sometimes I lay awake at night thinking that I ain't got too much time left on this earth, but I've had a good life and I don't mind it coming to an end, 'cause I'm tired, and the wife died years ago, and my boy went to the city of York and hasn't been back here for years."

A spasm of coughing interrupted his words. He pulled a dirty grey handkerchief from his pocket and wiped the spittle from his face.

"He never had any interest in the farm, anyways, only the money it will sell for when I'm dead and gone ... money that will line his pockets. He don't care about the farm or about Daisy, and I worry what will happen to her. The way things stand right now she'll be sold off with the farm, and who knows where she'll end up. She might go to someone who doesn't treat her right. I'd roll over in my grave if I thought she was being mistreated, or overworked.

"Next time I go to town, I'm gonna take myself to the lawyer's office and change my will. I can't think of a better person to leave my Daisy to than you. You and her are made for each other."

CHAPTER TWENTY-SIX

"Anyone here?" hollered the stranger, holding a white kerchief over his mouth and nose and peering tentatively into the barn, his eyes registering disgust at finding himself in such a place.

George climbed down the loft ladder.

"Who are you?" the stranger asked, taking a step back in alarm.

"I'm George, sir."

"What are you doing here?"

George took off his cap and kneaded it in his damp hands, his eyes focused on his moving knuckles. "I've been working for Mr. Clark goin' on a year. I do pretty much everything 'round here."

"Pack your things and be out by morning. The farm is being sold."

"Yes, sir. Me and Daisy will be on our way at first light."

"Who's Daisy? Your woman? Yes, take her, too. Both of you have to get out."

"Daisy's my horse. Mr. Clark said she'd be mine when he was gone, said he left her to me in his will."

The man consulted his notebook, adjusting wire-rimmed eyeglasses back and forth on his nose. "You mean the Clydesdale?"

George nodded.

"There's nothing in the will about leaving the horse to you."

"Mr. Clark said he was going to change the will and leave her to me, said he'd turn over in his grave if she gets sold to someone else."

"Well, he's rolling over now."

"What do you mean?"

"There's nothing in this will about leaving the horse to you. How long ago did he say he was going to change the will?"

"A month back, maybe more."

"This will is dated three years ago."

"But he changed it. He said the lawman would write it down."

The stranger unhooked the glasses from his ears. "I guess he never got around to it."

"He never wrote it down like he said he would?"

"No."

"But he gave me his word —"

"A man's word doesn't mean anything in this situation. It's not legal unless it's written down on paper, signed, and witnessed."

A memory flooded George's mind; he was a young boy again and a man with long hair talked to him in a language he did not understand and yet George knew exactly what the man was saying.

"Did you learn the scratchy lines?"

"Yes," George found himself saying aloud.

"Then, son, you will make sure we are not deceived again."

Anger blasted through George. He seethed with frustration. He knew how to read and write the white man's words, yet he had been deceived. He had failed! He wrung his cap in his hands, the only indication of the inner turmoil.

It's true, his inner voice screamed, *white men are not to be trusted. They are greedy and want everything for themselves.*

But even as he thought these things, he knew that Mr. Clark had not intended to trick him. The old man had wanted to write it down so there would be no dispute. He had wanted George to look after Daisy for the rest of her days. But time had run out for him. And now there was nothing George could do. He hung his head in despair.

"She's my family. What will happen to her?"

"She'll be auctioned off along with all the farm equipment."

"Sold?"

The man rolled his eyes. "That's generally what happens at an auction."

"How much?" George asked, excitedly. "I have money. I can buy her."

"Sure you can buy her. How much do you have?"

George rushed up the loft ladder and got a small leather pouch from under his mattress. All the coins he had been able to save since he had left school were in the bag. He loosened the drawstring and tipped the money into the man's hands.

"That's not enough to buy one leg," he scoffed. "She's a valuable animal. A champion. A good plough horse is hard to come by."

"Please, mister. I'll work to pay for her. I'll —"

The man tossed the money on the barn floor, the coins rolling away into dusty corners.

"I'll go with her," George continued, his voice taking on a tone of desperation. "The new owners will want someone to look after her and work her. I can handle the plough real good and the harrow and the hay wagon. I know how she likes her oats. Her tummy is real ticklish. You have to be careful when you brush her there or she'll kick. See, I know all these things —"

The man in the suit laughed. "You want to be sold with the horse?" He guffawed derisively. "That would sure stop the bidding!"

He turned and walked away. "If you're still here tomorrow I'll send the police over."

That night George tossed and turned, listening to Daisy in the stall beneath him. He thought about stealing her. He imagined climbing onto her back and riding away as fast and as far as possible, some place where nobody knew them, where nobody would follow them, where they could start a new life.

The spirit of hope made his heart race. *We could go north, where there are no white men.*

But despair rose up to crush hope almost as soon as it was born. *What will Daisy eat in the land of darkness and cold? She will starve without grass and hay and oats.*

Hope struggled to survive. *If we leave now, under the night sky, we could get away before they realize we have gone, before they start searching for us.*

The voice of reason spoke. *Daisy is too big to hide. People will see us. The police will catch us before we get out of the county.*

Hope refused to be trampled. *Unless we go now, right now. Right now!*

In the moonlight he led Daisy to the harness shed and bridled her, cutting the long driving reins to a more manageable length with his knife. He tied his blanket around his shoulders and Daisy's lead rope around her neck. Standing on the rickety step-ladder, he scrambled onto her back. She was warm beneath his legs, but he felt a little unsure of himself. He clucked and she moved forward with a surge that left him behind. He heaved on the reins. "Ho!"

Daisy stopped abruptly and they started over, this time more smoothly and they got to the end of the laneway without mishap. But doubt was speaking loudly in George's head. *The sun is already coming up. They will catch you. You'll go to jail.* A memory rose to the surface. He was imprisoned in a small wooden crate. He was cold and lonely and his limbs were cramped. He remembered a deer mouse that ran onto his lap to nibble the crumbs. He remembered how he had felt when the tiny creature scuttled away between the cracks and left him alone. He remembered hearing the lonely howl of a wolf. And then he remembered that his father had been hanged by the neck until he was dead.

Sitting on Daisy's warm broad back, he uttered a cry of despair into the dawn sky.

He turned the big horse around and took her back to her stall.

CHAPTER TWENTY-SEVEN

George walked away from the Clark farm and from Daisy. He had no idea where he should go. He fingered the wolf head pendant that nestled against his chest. As always, when he held the smooth piece of deer bone in his work-roughened hands, he felt something that bordered on sacred. He did not give thanks to Creator in the way of The People. Nor did he say the rote prayers he had learned in school. But he had a vague remembrance that once, a long time ago, the Spirit Wolves had helped him find his way home. He sent his thoughts through his fingertips. *Help me find a way.*

Gradually a seed of hope germinated in George's mind. The government, he had heard, sold land to settlers for next to nothing. That was the answer! A piece of land could provide him with food, water, and shelter, and free him from working for the white man.

He put on his school clothes, surprised to find that his arms and legs had grown longer and his chest broader since he had left school, and he went to the government office. Land, he was told, could only be sold to settlers: white men.

Indians could not buy land.

He was shooed from the office as though he was a flea-ridden dog, but as he was leaving, another government official pulled him aside

"You know you're entitled to treaty land, don't you? No strings attached. No charge."

George chuckled as he replied. "You mean the government is going to give me land of my own, and I don't even have to pay for it?"

"It's already yours."

George couldn't believe what he was hearing. "I won't have a boss telling me what to do or what to grow?"

The government official smiled. "That's right. You can be your own boss. You can grow whatever pleases you. You can cut timber and build a house. You can do whatever your heart desires. You can sit and drink whisky all day, and watch the trees grow, if that's what you want. I hear that's what most of them do up there."

George couldn't help but sense that there was some loophole or condition that he had not, as yet, understood. "Are you sure about this?"

"I'm sure. You're a *Status* Indian —"

George had been called many names in his life, but this was new.

"— and it means you're on the list."

"List?"

"The status list."

George's face was blank.

"You were counted by the government and they put you on their list. The word *Status* means *Legal Status*. It means you're *legally* an Indian."

George had a fleeting thought of Mother Hall trying to make him an English boy. Even then he doubted they would ever let him be one! Here was the proof. He was legally an Indian.

"Being *Status* gives you rights," the official continued.

"What rights?" George asked, shocked to hear that he had any.

"The right to live on the reserve, for one, and own your own plot of land."

George's spirits sank. That was the catch! He had to go back to the reserve.

"If you were *Non-status* you wouldn't have those rights," the man explained. "You'd have nothing!"

George mind raced.

Going back to the reserve is taking a step in the wrong direction! the educated George thought.

But I want my own land, more than anything in the world, his heart protested.

The people on the reserve are sinful. If you go back you'll be no better than them. You'll go back to their level.

George's heart was not to be silenced. *But I want the freedom that land will give me.*

The reasoning part of George was quick to counter. *You endured ten years in that school, to rise above the disadvantage of your birth, so that you could have a better life than the old Indians. You can't go back! You are educated. You are better than the savages on the reserve.*

Who says?

The teachers at school.

It seems to me, George said with his whole heart, *that school didn't help me much. Getting educated and learning to be like them didn't do me much good.*

The opposing voice was silent.

The sound of bells pealed across the farmland. Conflicting thoughts still troubled George. It was Sunday morning and he felt pulled toward the unassuming white clapboard building, yet repelled by it at the same time. He wanted to connect with the God-Man, but he didn't want to see or be seen by the white-skins who were arriving at the church in their traps and wagons.

The congregation was singing a hymn as George pushed open the heavy wooden door and slipped into the empty back pew.

"All ye in Christ draw near in faith, one brother-hood of man...."

No one noticed George at first. He glanced around, his eyes settling on the figurine that hung on the wall: a crucified man with fair hair, blue eyes, and skin paler than even the palest white-skin. George was confused. The God-Man at school had had long brown hair, brown eyes, and skin the colour of a white man's summer tan.

They've killed another one!

George felt as though he had been punched in the chest. He gasped.

A worshipper turned around and whispered to her companions. The singing died away until the pianist alone carried the tune. The old familiar feel-ings rose again; his heart pounded in his chest, his palms tingled with sweat, and his stomach lurched.

The pianist stopped playing.

George rose to his feet and, willing himself not to run, pushed open the big door and walked away.

His mind was numb, almost vacant, the way it often was when these things happened, but then a voice sounded in his head.

Live The True Life.

"What do you mean?" George asked

Find the old ones. Learn their ways.

George reached for the wolf head pendant and caressed it with his fingertips. *Do you mean I should go back to the reserve? Is this the way you have found for me ... the path upon which I should tread?*

There was no reply.

A wry smile lit his face. He had spent his whole life learning how to become part of a society that didn't want him. He had been taught to despise his own people, and now here he was, caught between two cultures, fitting in nowhere. But he was no longer captive to the school's teaching or punishment. He was free to return to his roots and to his wicked ways. He could learn the old language and the old ways, perhaps find some wisdom and make some sense out of life. At school they had taught him he was uncivilized and unchristian. But he had found nothing civilized or Christian in them. They spoke of love; Christian love; brotherly love; the love of God. But they were filled with hate!

And greed.

They destroyed everything around them.

CHAPTER TWENTY-EIGHT

George was shocked when he saw his mother. She bore no resemblance to the faded image he had in his mind. Of course she had aged, but it was more than that. There was no light in her eyes. Her hair hung in matted strands and her skin was sallow. She smelled of alcohol and sweat. StarWoman was not unique. There were many others on the reserve just like her.

At first she didn't accept that George was her son. He too had changed, and even when he convinced her that he really was *Mishqua Ma'een'gun*, she refused to call him George, but that was fine with the young man. George wanted to learn from the elders, and since none of them spoke English, George needed to improve his *Anishnaabemowin*.

Almost a year passed before he felt confident enough with the language to ask his mother about his father's death.

"The government man came here that spring to register more children for school," StarWoman said. "Lali had not even seen four summers! Your father told the man that she was too young, that she must stay with us one more year. But the agent said your father was wrong, that Lali must go to school in September. HeWhoWhistles went crazy!

"The man had a fire-stick. This was not the first time your father had looked into its mouth."

Red Wolf was surprised. "When was the first?"

"Do you not remember? It was when the white man said you must go to their school."

Red Wolf had forgotten the incident that happened so long ago, but his mother's words jogged his memory and a picture came to his mind.

"Were you screaming and fighting the white man?" he asked.

"Yes!"

"And did they almost shoot Father in the back?"

"Yes! The man was going to shoot *me*. Your father covered me with his body so the burning stone would hit him, not me. He was very brave. In the end, the white man walked away without firing ... perhaps the Ancestors heard our prayers.

"Your father protected me that day, but he could not protect you! You went away to Bruce County School. He never forgave himself. It was the biggest regret of his life ... that he could not protect you."

Red Wolf felt shaky inside.

"When the white man came to register Lali for school and your father saw the fire-stick, he acted fast. He knocked it from the man's hand with a swift kick, so he could fight the man on equal terms. The man was bigger than your father, but anger gave your father strength. He was fighting against all of the injustices that had been forced upon us, the loss of our land, and especially the loss of you, *Mishqua Ma'een'gun.*

"Before long, the man lay on his back, groaning. Your father picked up the government fire-stick. He pointed it at the man's head. He held it there a long time. Long enough for us all to see terror in the white man's eyes; long enough to hear him beg and plead for his life; long enough for us to smell the stench as his bowels released. And then your father pulled the trigger."

Red Wolf felt as if he was hit in the gut with a club. Did his father kill the Indian agent, the one who had intimidated him and called him Horse Thief? He tried to remember the last time he had seen the man. It was before Father Thomas had told him that his father had been hanged.

"The man that Father killed —" he said, almost scared to ask the question "— was he the man who called me Horse Thief?"

"Yes, of course. You didn't know that?"

Red Wolf was astounded. He barely heard the rest of the words his mother spoke.

"Your father waited for the police to arrive on their horses," StarWoman continued, her voice quivering. "He didn't try to run away and hide. He gave himself up without a fight, admitting that he had killed the man. They took him away and I never saw him again. All these years and it still hurts me."

She pulled herself together. "I found out later that the lawmen did not speak *Anishnaabemowin*, or even Algonquian. They spoke to your father only in their tongue. HeWhoWhistles had wanted people to know why he had killed the man. But the lawmen couldn't understand his words, so his voice was never heard.

"And of course Lali still had to go away to school. I haven't seen her since the day they took her from here. They said they were giving her to a white family because I was a drunk." The words caught in her throat. "I don't know where she is."

George wanted to hold his mother and comfort her, but he had learned to deny his emotions a long time ago. He turned from her and walked away. He was outside the cabin when he heard her wail. The high-pitched keening tore at his heart and although he didn't rush back inside and hold her in his arms, his own tears started to fall. He walked into the bush and wailed.

Years earlier, when Father Thomas had told him that his father was dead, he had not mourned the way he did now. The grief shocked and bewildered him. He felt as if someone had reached inside and grabbed a vital part of him, tearing it away and leaving an open wound. He had always believed that HeWhoWhistles had not loved him enough to fight for him, and now the truth was almost too much to bear.

He imagined his father swinging at the end of a hangman's noose. He doubled over and gagged. "How could they do that to you? How could they take your life like that?"

George shuddered.

George had planned to farm the treaty land that was rightfully his. He needed a few tools to get started: a saw to clear land, and a plough, and harrow. He didn't need an expensive horse like Daisy, just an old work pony or a mule. He'd been told that farmers could buy agricultural equipment with an interest-free government loan. George straightened the wrinkles out of his old school clothes once again and polished his boots. With bare wrists sticking out from the jacket, bare ankles protruding past the trouser legs, and buttons that were severely strained across his chest, he went to the bank. He was told to get out before the police were called. Indians were not allowed to apply for loans.

Soon George was no different from the dispirited people on the reserve, numbed from reality by alcohol, sleeping until noon. He had no friends, not even among those who had also suffered the residential school experience. They were men and women living lives of individual pain, with spouses they didn't know how to love, and babies they didn't know how to nurture.

And each September more children were taken away.

One evening George was talking with a newly arrived graduate from Bruce County Indian School. Within seconds George knew that he didn't like him. He was too disdainful of the people on the reserve.

"I'm not going to be here long," the young man explained. "I'm going as far as I can from this god-forsaken place, perhaps to York."

"Why did you come back here, then?"

"To try, one more time, to get Mother to accept Jesus."

George laughed. "Father Thomas is still giving the boys that job, eh?"

"Yes," the young man replied seriously. "Mother has resisted the gospel all these years, but she's not well. Who knows how much longer she has."

George's humour was thinly disguised by his solemn and urgent demeanour. "You must save her before she goes to the Hell-*wiigwam*!"

The young man missed George's cynicism. "That's right," he answered. "The only way our folks are going to be saved is if *we* save them. Evil is all around them here. Just today I heard about this very old woman who lives deep in the forest. She shuffles around banging a hand drum and singing, if you can call it that. She howls like a wolf to the full moon! She eats roots and leaves and berries. Lives in a *wiigwam* like a real old style Indian!" He guffawed derisively. "The old crone thinks she's Medicine Woman!"

George didn't hear the boy's scathing laughter. In his mind he was at his grandmother's side, his tiny hand engulfed by hers, walking through the deep forest, searching for plants that made good medicine, sniffing for herbs to season meat and make tea, digging roots to dye porcupine quills, collecting acorns.

"Who is she, this Medicine Woman?" George asked.

"The mother of that man who was hanged years back."

George's heart skipped a beat. "Are you sure?"

"Yes. They say she lost her mind after the hanging. She went into the forest and never came back. She lives like a wild animal, a savage."

George rushed back to his mother's cabin to question her about the grandmother he had assumed was dead.

StarWoman was dismissive. "The mother of HeWhoWhistles has not been seen for many winters," she said. "She is surely in the Spirit World, with HeWhoWhistles and Grandfather and the Ancestors."

"People have seen her! She is still alive!"

"I think not, *Mishqua Ma'een'gun.*"

Grandmother was alive! George knew it. "Where is her *wiigwam*? Do you know?"

StarWoman closed her eyes and George waited, hoping she would say more, but soon her head lolled onto her chest and she snored quietly.

George wanted to shake his mother awake, but he sat patiently and gazed out the open door. Suddenly a dog stood in the doorway. There were several dogs on the reserve. Some looked like wolves and were the result of cross breeding between the wild and the tame. But this one was different. George didn't recognize the animal and yet there was something familiar about the thick mottled grey undercoat, the long guard hairs of burnished red, the bushy tail, and the amber eyes.

He walked toward the dog, speaking soft words of greeting. The animal sniffed his outstretched hand and licked it. George dropped to one knee and sank his fingertips into the thick fur. Memories started to rise: memories of a wolf who was once his friend. The feelings were disturbing. George could feel his heart expanding in his chest. He didn't know what to do.

He stood back and looked at the dog. Both ears were pointed upward like two triangles, but then he cocked his head to one side. With a faint yip and a look of curiosity on his face, the left ear bent in half and keeled forward.

Tears pooled in George's eyes, spilling over and coursing down his cheeks. There was nothing he could do to stop them. He threw his arms around the dog's neck and buried his face in the thick, warm fur.

And he remembered.

He remembered the way he had felt when he had buried his face in Crooked Ear's fur. He remembered his mother, the way she had been, not as she was now, her excitement the day he had stopped paddling the canoe in circles and propelled it in a straight line. She had jumped up and down, beaming with pride.

He remembered spearing his first fish and hearing his father cheer.

George's tears flowed into the dog's fur. He had never cried tears like these. Eventually he raised his head and the dog licked the salt from his tear-stained face.

He felt different, as though part of him was dying. But at the same time he was alive in an unusually vibrant way. In a flash, he knew exactly what was happening.… George was leaving! George would soon be gone! And *Mishqua Ma'een'gun* was returning.

He kissed his sleeping mother lightly on her brow, tucked the wolf head pendant safely inside his shirt and headed to the door.

"I'm going to find Grandmother," he told the dog. "Do you want to come with me?"

The dog bounded ahead.

Red Wolf smiled and shouted after him. "Do you have a name?"

The dog paused and looked back, his left ear flopping in half.

In the language of The People, a name sounded loudly in Red Wolf's head.

Son of Crooked Ear.

THE PEOPLE

The *Anishnaabe* nation has lived in the vast forests of the Great Lakes region for thousands of years. In their own language (*Anishnaabemowen*) the word *Anishnaabe* (plural *Anishnaabek*) means *The True People*. To the rest of the world they are more commonly and collectively known as Ojibwey (Ojibway, Ojibwe, Ojibwa). This is the name they were given by others.

Prior to European contact, historians estimate that between 500,000 and 2 million people lived in what we now know as Canada, just a small percentage of the estimated 100 million who lived in the Americas. Spread over an enormous landmass, belonging to many tribes and nations, speaking different languages and dialects, these Canadian indigenous people shared a remarkably similar fundamental worldview. Their way of life was firmly rooted in the relationship to their Creator, the environment, and all living things. They shared their possessions, respected their elders, loved their children, and governed by democratic council. They were good custodians of the land, water, and resources that sustained them. Yet Europeans of the time regarded the Indians as savages who occupied valuable land, and who, for their own good, needed to be converted to Christianity.

The Canadian government decided to solve the "Indian problem" by assimilation. The *Gradual Civilization Act* of 1857 laid the foundation, followed by the *British North America Act* in 1867, and the *Indian Act* of 1876 that legalized and detailed the Canadian government's system for controlling and assimilating Aboriginal peoples. Sections 113 to 122 of the *Indian Act* legally took away the rights of parents, giving the government total control of the children. And for more than a hundred years, Royal Canadian Mounted Police enforced the law, authorizing and enabling government employees, known as Indian agents, to remove children from their homes and incarcerate them in residential schools, sometimes hundreds of miles away.

Between 1840 and 1984, when the last school closed, 100,000 First Nations children had passed through, or died in, the Canadian residential school system. During the peak years of the mid-twentieth century, there were 76 residential schools across Canada. The government delegated the day-to-day running of the schools to four major churches: Roman Catholic, Church of England, Presbyterian, and United. The government paid the churches a stipend for each child. The churches were thus empowered to change Indian culture without societal checks or balances. This freedom set the scene for blatant abuse.

Not all children were abused in the now infamous residential schools, although in the twenty-first century, when the silence is finally being broken, it appears that many were. But even those who were treated with kindness still experienced traumatic separation from family, community, language, and culture that had far-reaching effects. The government's policy was, in effect, cultural genocide.

Native American children in the United States endured a similar fate. Between 1878 and 1930, as part of the U.S. Government's Indian Policy, children were taken from their families and sent to boarding schools to be educated mostly by missionaries. As in Canada, these children were given new names, were forbidden to use their own language, and were taught Christian, European-American culture. They received only a basic education that focused on manual skills.

In 2008 Canada's prime minister, Stephen Harper, made an apology to former students of the residential school system. "The treatment of children in Indian residential schools is a sad chapter in our history. Today, we recognize that this policy of assimilation was wrong, has caused great harm, and has no place in our country. The government now recognizes that the consequences of the Indian residential schools policy were profoundly negative and that this policy has had a lasting and damaging impact on aboriginal culture, heritage and language."

Bruce County Indian Residential School does not exist, nor to my knowledge did it ever exist. The school depicted in this story is a fictional amalgamation of many schools across Canada, based on the experiences and memories of First Peoples. Similarly, the characters are fictional.

THE WOLVES

Before white settlers arrived on North American shores, timber wolves, *Canis lupus*, also known as grey wolves, hunted the vast ancestral range of the entire landmass. They lived in highly social family groups and co-existed with nature in a delicate dance of survival. To the Europeans, the wolves, like the indigenous people, were viewed as dangerous and savage. They occupied land that the settlers wanted. Wolves were systematically shot, trapped, snared, and poisoned, enabling the settlers to log and cultivate the land, and to raise livestock. If the wolf was to survive in this new era, he had little choice. He had to run to places where the white man could not follow. Today, North America's timber wolves live almost exclusively in Northern Canada and Alaska, far from human habitation. But in the twentieth century, wolves were not even safe in these remote wilderness areas. Hunters shot wolves ruthlessly from airplanes and dropped poison bait into formerly inaccessible places. In 1972 Ontario finally put an end to bounty payments, but hunting wolves was still legal.

Interestingly, the Algonquin Wolves found today in Ontario's wilderness sanctuary of the same name are *not* timber wolves. They are red wolves, *Canis rufus*. After the loggers cleared the forests in the Algonquin area and had killed or driven away the timber wolf and the elk, their main source of food, white-tailed deer, started to flourish and with it the smaller red wolf, which had already been extirpated in the southeastern United States. Red wolves, like their bigger grey cousins, were also hunted, almost to extinction, but Algonquin Park became their sanctuary. However, when wolves left the protection of the park's fenceless perimeter, they were still hunted, and their survival remained in jeopardy.

In 2003, the Canadian government permanently banned hunting in the townships surrounding the park.

A NOTE ON LANGUAGE

The Ojibwey language, with its many divergent dialects, is spoken throughout the Great Lakes region and westward onto the northern plains. It is one of the largest American Indian languages north of Mexico. Due to the long history and large geographical area there are many ways to pronounce and, in recent times, write the language. The newest Roman character-based writing system is the Double Vowel system devised by Charles Fiero. Because of its ease of use the Fiero system is quickly gaining popularity among language teachers in the United States and Canada.

ACKNOWLEDGEMENTS

I owe an enormous debt of gratitude to Marilyn Paxton Deline of First Nations Creations who saw some merit in my first draft and worked with me to ensure the Anishnaabe, their language, beliefs, and culture were accurately represented. And also to Judith Ennamorato for her enthusiastic response to my writing, and for her book, *Sing the Brave Song*, a comprehensive scrutiny of the relationship between Indian people and the church and the repercussions endured by former students of the residential school system. Judith's book was invaluable in writing *Red Wolf*.

I would also like to thank Feroze Mohammed. For teaching me to be a better writer, from punctuation, spelling and sentence structure, to sharing your knowledge of the subject matter and remaining on track with the story. For the countless hours that you spent on this project, I thank you. I could not have done it without you.

Warm thank-yous to:

Jason Robertson for loving my daughter and opening the door to the telling of this story; Erin Robertson for sharing her research and personal stories about residential school life that fuelled my desire to write this book; Dianne Robertson for her prayers, her conviction that this story needed to be told, and her belief that I, a non-native, could tell it; Jane Warren for her willingness to read yet another version of the book and for her insightful suggestions that helped me to develop a better story; Heather Cargill for reading *Red Wolf* with the senior class of Uxbridge Montessori school; Darlene Campbell and Betty Scuse for their spiritual insight and friendship; Educators Gail Aziz, Susan Hayward, Doris Beers, Lydia Keen, Pat Dipede, Georgina Wolske, Robert Lawrence, Margaret, and Shiraz Mohammed for sharing their wisdom about the target audience. And most importantly, my middle-grade readers: Persia Mahdavi, Decara Adams, Lorelei Adams, Maggie Anderson, Liam Banks-Batten, Liam Burns-Holland, Ciaran Conlan, Siobhan Conlan, Charlotte Damus, Elena Damus, Madeleine Galloway, Karter Hickling, GJaudy John-Wallace, Sam Keen, Chris Menard, Jon Menard, Erik Morris, Siena Morris, Justine Simpson, Clayton Tennakoon, and Maverick Worgan.

I also want to thank Jim Brandenburg for the amazing photography and narrative in his book,

Brother Wolf: A Forgotten Promise. Jim's outstanding work following wolves in the wild helped me find Crooked Ear in my imagination and make him real.

My heartfelt thanks go to Allister Thompson at Dundurn for his enthusiastic response to the manuscript at a time when other publishers were shying away from this sensitive subject.

And last, but not least, I thank my children: Joanna, James, Kate, Tarik, and Matthew. You have blessed my life in ways you cannot fathom. I could not have written this book, without you! I first learned about Indian residential schools when you were heading out into the big wide world of elementary school. I was unable to imagine the pain of other mothers whose little ones were ripped away for ten long months each year It weighed on my heart. *Red Wolf* is the result.

MORE FICTION FROM DUNDURN

Broken Circle
by Christopher Dinsdale
978-1894917155
$8.95

Angry at missing a week of summer video game entertainment, Jesse, a twelve-year-old boy of European/Native American descent, grudgingly follows through with his deceased father's request that he join his Uncle Matthew and cousin Jason at Six Islands, on Georgian Bay, for a special camping trip. Uncle Matthew explains that Jesse's late father wanted Jason's vision quest to be his introduction to their culture. During their first night around the campfire, it is Jesse who has a vision, and the adventure begins. Not only is he swept back in time four hundred years, but he is transformed into a majestic, white-tailed deer. He must now survive the expert hunting skills of his ancestors while somehow rescuing his people before they are destroyed by warfare.

I Am Algonquin
by Rick Revelle
978-1459707184
$12.99

Painting a vivid picture of the original peoples of North America before the arrival of Europeans, *I Am Algonquin* follows the story of Mahingan and his family as they live the traditional Algonquin way of life in what is now Ontario in the early fourteenth century. Along the way we learn about the search for moose and the dramatic rare woodland buffalo hunt, conflicts with other Native nations, and the dangers of wolves and wolverines. We also witness the violent game of lacrosse, the terror of a forest fire, and the rituals that allow Algonquin boys to be declared full-grown men.

But warfare is also part of their lives, and signs point to a defining conflict between Mahingan's nation, its allies the Omàmiwinini (Algonquin), Ouendat (Huron), and the Nippissing against the Haudenosaunee (Iroquois). The battle's aftermath may open the door to future journeys by Mahingan and his followers.

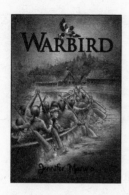

Warbird
by Jennifer Maruno
978-1926607115
$9.95

In 1647, ten-year-old Etienne yearns for a life of adventure far from his family farm in Quebec. He meets an orphan destined to apprentice among the Jesuits at Fort Sainte-Marie. Making the most impulsive decision of his life, Etienne replaces the orphan and paddles off with the voyageurs into the north country. At Sainte-Marie, Etienne must learn to live a life of piety. Meanwhile, he also makes friends with a Huron youth, Tsiko, who teaches him the ways of his people. When the Iroquois attack and destroy the nearby village, Etienne must put his new skills into practice. Will he survive? Will he ever see his family again?

Available at your favourite bookseller

VISIT US AT
Dundurn.com
@dundurnpress
Facebook.com/dundurnpress
Pinterest.com/dundurnpress